P9-ECK-672

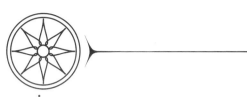

This special signed edition is limited to 500 numbered copies.

This is copy **425**.

THE RIVER HORSES

THE RIVER HORSES

Allen Steele

SUBTERRANEAN PRESS 2007

First Edition

ISBN
978-1-59606-132-3

Subterranean Press
PO Box 190106
Burton, MI 48519

www.subterraneanpress.com

The shed's wooden doors rumbled as they were pushed apart by a couple of proctors. Early morning sun flooded the barnlike interior, causing Marie to raise a hand to her eyes. About thirty yards away, her brother walked up the dirt path that would lead him back to town. For a moment she thought Carlos would turn to wave goodbye, but he'd turned his back upon her, and there was nothing more to be said between them.

The proctors finished opening the vehicle shed. Neither of them spoke as they turned toward her, but the one on the left tucked the thumb in his gun belt, his hand only a few inches from the butt of his holstered flechette pistol, while his companion nodded toward the skimmer parked behind her. A wayward grasshoarder fluttered into the building; Marie's eyes followed the small bird as it alighted upon the floodlight rack mounted above the glass hemisphere of the hovercraft's cockpit. Then Lars started the twin duct-fan engines; alarmed by the abrupt roar, the grasshoarder flew away.

"Time to go, Ms. Montero." Manny loaded the last crate of supplies aboard the skimmer; grasping the hatch-bar of the starboard cargo bin and pulling it shut, the savant walked over to her. "We have to leave."

Marie didn't respond. Instead, she glanced back toward where she'd last seen Carlos, only to find that her brother had already disappeared into the tall grass that lay between Sand Creek and Liberty. She'd expected him to watch her leave, at least; finding that he wasn't going to do even this, she felt something cold close around her heart.

"Ms. Montero..."

Something touched her left shoulder; looking around, she saw that Manny had laid one of his clawlike hands upon her. "Get away from me," she snapped as she tried to swat it away. The four-fingered claw was made of ceramic carbon, though, and was hard as steel. Flesh met unresisting metal, and she winced in pain.

"Sorry." As always, the savant's face registered no emotion; it was only a silver skull, a death's head shrouded by the raised hood of his black cloak. His remaining eye, the right one, emitted a faint amber hue; the left one was covered by a patch. His hand disappeared within the folds of his robe. "I didn't mean to..."

"Just stay away, all right?" Marie had spent the last several years of her life learning how to hate Manuel Castro; just because he'd volunteered to accompany her and Lars didn't give her any reason to make friends now. Massaging her fingertips, she stepped around him and marched toward the skimmer. Within the cockpit, Lars waited for her, his face impassive as he kept the engines at idle. Marie glanced up at him and he gave her a quiet nod. No point in standing around, and they had no choice; it was time to go.

She was about to mount the ladder to the skimmer's middeck when Chris Levin came up behind her. "Marie..."

She paused, her hands on the ladder's bottom rung. The Chief Proctor held out a satphone, wrapped in a waterproof catskin packet. "In case the com system goes down," he said, his voice barely audible above the muttering engines. "Don't use it unless..."

He stopped, not needing to finish the rest: *Unless you're in so much trouble that you can't get yourselves out of it. Then we might come get you, but only if it's a life or death situation. Otherwise, you're on your own.*

She wondered if he was embarrassed by what was happening here. After all, he himself had been made an outcast once, many years ago. Marie took the satphone, hooked it to her belt. She thought to say something, then realized that any words from her would be pointless. Behind Chris, another proctor watched her; his eyes were hidden by a pair of sunglasses, yet his expression was unkind. Not wanting to give anyone the satisfaction of hearing her beg forgiveness, she simply nodded. Chris gave her a tight-lipped smile, then offered his hand. Marie chose to ignore the gesture, though; the last thing she wanted was belated sympathy from her brother's best friend. Turning away from them, she grasped the ladder rungs and climbed up onto the skimmer.

The top hatch was open; she climbed down into it and, ducking her head, clambered through the narrow aft compartment into the cockpit. The skimmer was an Armadillo AC-IIb, a light assault vehicle left behind by the Union Guard after the Revolution; there were four seats within the bubble, two forward for the pilot and co-pilot, two in back for the gunner and engineer. The 30mm chain gun and rocket launchers had been removed, though, and only a few capped wires showed where the weapons-control panel had been dismantled. Seeing this, she wondered whether the skimmer's armament had been taken out before now, or if the magistrates had decided that they didn't want to risk giving her and Lars enough firepower to level most of the colony. She wasn't sure she wanted to know the answer.

"Ready to go?" Lars glanced over his shoulder at her. Marie didn't say anything as she squeezed past him, making her way toward the bucket seat on the right forward side. "Okay, then let's go."

"You're not forgetting someone, are you?" Castro's leaden footfalls had been lost in the growl of the idling engines; Marie looked around to see the savant's head and shoulders emerge through the hatch leading to the aft compartment. "I'd be insulted if you did."

Lars didn't reply, yet his hands fell from the control yoke and his head fell back on his neck. "I wouldn't be...never mind." Then he turned to look at the savant. "Look, we're going to get along fine if you'll just keep your mouth shut."

"My mouth *is* shut, Mr. Thompson." Castro's voice emerged from the vocoder grille on the lower part of his face. "I wouldn't have it any other way...and you?"

Lars slowly let out his breath. He turned back around, but when he grasped the yoke again, Marie noticed that the knuckles of his hands were white. "Keep pushing it," he murmured. "Just keep pushing it..."

"Let's just go, okay?" Through the curved panes of the canopy, she could see the proctors watching them, their hands never far from their sidearms. Chris had stepped away from the vehicle; she briefly met his eye, and saw that any vestige of their childhood friendship had been lost behind an implacable mask of authority. Suddenly, she was sick of Liberty, and everyone who lived here. "C'mon. I just want to get out of this place."

A grim smile crept across Lars' face. "Your wish is my command." He reached to the twin throttle bars, gently slid them upward. The engines revved to a higher pitch, and the hovercraft rose upon its inflatable pontoons and began to ease forward...and then, obeying a sudden, violent impulse, Lars shoved the bars the rest of the way into high gear.

"Hang on!" he yelled, as the skimmer lunged for the shed doors.

The proctors standing at the entrance were caught by surprise. For a moment, they simply stared at them in shock, then they threw themselves out of the way. Marie caught a brief glimpse of the proctor to the right as he tripped over a barrel and fell to the concrete floor. For a moment, she thought Lars would run over him, but the proctor managed to scramble out of the way before the Armadillo swept out of the shed.

"*Yeee-haaah!*" Lars's rebel yell reverberated within the cockpit, almost drowning out the engines. "Run, you son-of-a-bitches! *Run!*"

Once the skimmer was clear of the shed, he twisted the yoke hard to the right, aiming for the nearby creek.

Pieces of grass and flecks of mud spattered the bottom part of the bubble; Marie clung to her armrests as her body whiplashed back and forth in her seat.

"Gangway!" Lars shouted. "Mad driver! Run for your...!"

"Stop it!" Marie reached forward, grabbed the throttle bars. "Stop it right now!"

She yanked the throttle back in neutral. The back end of the skimmer lifted slightly as it coasted to a halt, less than a half-dozen yards from the creek. Though the tall grass, she caught sight of a canoe drifting near the shore; two teenagers, neither much younger than she or Lars, stared at them in horror, their fishing poles still clutched in their hands. In another second or two, Lars would have mowed them down.

Lars's laughter died, the ugly amusement in his eyes suddenly turning to frustrated anger. "You said you wanted to get out of here," he said, grabbing her hand and trying to pry it away from the throttles. "I was just doing like you..."

"That's not what I meant!" Wincing against his grasp, she wrapped her fingers more firmly around the bars. "I don't want to leave this way," she added, speaking more softly now. "I just want to..." *I want to come back some day when no one is afraid of me anymore, or at least when my own brother can look me in the eye.* "Just take it easy," she finished, struggling for words that might get through to him. "Show a little class, y'know what I mean?"

Dull comprehension crept across her boyfriend's face. "Yeah, sure," he murmured. He released his grip from her hand, and it wasn't until then that she realized how much he'd hurt her. "Just take it easy," he said, repeating what she'd said as if the idea was his own. "Show a little class."

"That's it." Marie let go of the throttles. "Be cool. That'll really bug 'em."

The outlaw smirk reappeared on Lars's face. He laid his right hand on the throttles again, and for a moment Marie thought he'd jam them forward once more. But instead he eased the bars up just a half-inch, and the skimmer responded by sluggishly moving forward. The teenagers in the canoe had already paddled out of range by the time the Armadillo entered the narrow river; there was a mild splash as the pontoons drove water against the cockpit, rinsing away torn-up grass and mud.

"So," Lars asked, "which way you want to go?"

"To...." Marie hesitated. "I don't know." She pointed downstream, south from where they where now. "That way, at least until I can get our bearings."

"Our bearings?" He glanced at her. "What, you don't know where you are? I mean..."

"Just go that way, okay?"

She pushed herself out of her seat. Castro's skeletal face raised slightly as she brushed against him; for a brief instant, as the multifaceted ruby of his right eye gleamed at her, she caught dozens of tiny reflections of herself, each tinted the color of diluted blood. Yet the savant said nothing as she ducked her head to make her way through the aft-section hatch, and anything else Lars might have said to her was lost in the thrum of the skimmer's engines.

The day was a little older when she climbed out through the topside hatch. Grasping the slender handrails, she stood upon the middeck, feeling the engines vibrating beneath the soles of her boots as she gazed back the way the way they'd just come. The wood-shingled rooftops of Liberty were already lost to her; she caught a last glimpse of the grange hall, the tall mast of its adjacent weather tower rising above the treetops. A minute later, the faux-birch cabins and shops of Shuttlefield went by; the shadow of Swamp Road Bridge fell across her, and Marie looked up to see a little girl, not much older than she herself had been when she'd come to Coyote, waving to her from its railing. Marie lifted her hand to wave back, and the girl beamed at her, delighted to be acknowledged by a woman traveling down Sand Creek, bound for glories that she could only imagine.

Marie stood on the deck until the last vestiges of human civilization disappeared behind her. Then, wiping tears from her eye with the back of her hand, she climbed back down the hatch.

From the journal of
Wendy Gunther:
Uriel 47, c.y. 06

Today was First Landing Day, our first since the Revolution. I should be happy, but it's hard for me to join the celebration: we sent Marie and Lars into exile today.

That's not the official term, of course. The magistrates are calling it "corrective banishment," and claim that it's a more benign form of punishment than sentencing them to a year in the stockade. Perhaps this bends Colony Law a bit, but count on Carlos to come up with a new idea; he didn't want to see Marie do hard time, so he used his mayoral influence to convince the maggies that his sister and her boyfriend would benefit from being sent to explore the wilderness. And since Marie and Lars are former members of the Rigil Kent brigade, no one wanted to put a couple of war vets on the road crew. Better for them to do something that might serve the community more than digging ditches and hauling gravel.

I thought Clark Thompson would object. After all, he's not only a member of the Colonial Council, but Lars is also his nephew. From what I gather, he and his wife Molly raised Lars and his brother Garth as their own children after their parents were killed (never got the full story on that—wonder what happened?). But Clark is as tough as Molly is gentle, and he was furious when he learned that his boy held a man's arms behind his back while Marie slashed his face with a broken bottle, the outcome of a tavern brawl that should have been settled with fists and nothing worse. Like Carlos, Clark figured that statutory reform was preferable to penal time, so he agreed not to stand in the way while the magistrates sent Lars and Marie into exile...pardon me, "corrective banishment."

They may be right. Marie and Lars aren't hardened criminals, nor are they sociopaths (or at least Marie isn't—I'm not too sure about Lars). Yet the fact remains that both of them came into adulthood fighting a guerilla war against Union forces. In a better world, Marie would have spent her adolescence knitting sweaters and fidgeting in school, while Lars might have done nothing more harmful than pestering the neighbors with homemade stink bombs. But they were deprived of that sort of idyllic fantasy; they grew up with rifles in their hands, learning how to shoot enemy soldiers from a hundred yards away with no more remorse than killing a swamper. Their first date should have been a shy kiss and a furtive grope behind the grange hall, not a quick screw somewhere in occupied territory, with one eye on the woods and their weapons within arm's reach.

So this morning, just before sunrise, Chris had his proctors release them from the stockade. They were marched down to the vehicle shed, where they were given a decommissioned Union Guard skimmer, along with rifles, ammo, wilderness gear, and enough food to last

them a month. And then Carlos told them to get lost...
literally. Go out and explore the boonies, and don't come
back for six months. If they show up in any of the other
colonies—Defiance, Forest Camp, New Boston—they'll
be arrested and sent back here to serve out the rest of
their sentence, plus six months, in the stockade. Until
then, they're expected to survey the wilderness and use
the skimmer's satphone to make a report every couple of
days or so on what they've found.

I have to hand it to my husband: as solutions go, it's not
such a bad one. The Union occupation pretty much fore-
stalled further exploration of Coyote, or at least beyond
what we found on Midland while we were hiding from
the Union. Once the Revolution ended, we had our hands
full, dealing with the climatic after-effects of the Mt.
Bonestell eruption. So nearly eight-tenths of this world
have never been seen except from space; the maps we
have, for the most part, are little more than composites of
low-orbit photos.

Time to send out the scouts, even if they're con-
scripts. Carlos spent several months alone on the Great
Equatorial River, so he knows it's possible to live off the
land. And I know how he changed for the better from
that experience. He left Liberty as an irresponsible, reck-
less boy, and came back as the man I was willing to marry
and be the father of my child, Why not have his sister and
her boyfriend have the same benefit?

And it isn't as if they're completely on their own.
Manny Castro has volunteered to go with them. To be
sure, this is a calculated risk. Manny isn't just a savant—

he was also the lieutenant governor of Liberty during the Union occupation. Lars even attempted to drown him after he was captured during the Thompson's Ferry massacre. But Manny is trying to find his place in the world, I think, now that the Matriarch is gone and the Union has fled Coyote…and perhaps Lars should learn what it's like to live with someone whom he once tried to murder.

So it's all very logical, all very sane, all very benign. Everything we've done today is in keeping with the sort of society we aspire to create on this world. And yet…I'm still not certain whether we've done the right thing. We can justify our actions with our choice of words, yet the fact remains that we've just sent three people into exile.

I've never been much of a religious person. My faith is in the human spirit, not in what most people call God. Nonetheless, if there are angels in the heavens, I pray that they guard and protect those whom we've made outcasts.

They made camp late that afternoon downstream from Liberty, on a brush-covered spit of land formed by the divergence of Levin Creek from Sand Creek. This was boid country; they were near the place where, four Coyote years ago, Jim Levin and Gil Reese has lost their lives in a fateful hunting expedition. Marie knew the story well; Carlos had been on that same trip, back when he was a teenager. She was reluctant to spend the night there, but Lars was nonchalant about the risk they were taking.

"Look, we've got rifles," he said, "and we've got *it*." He pointed to Manny, who'd undertaken the task of unloading their gear from the skimmer, now floating next to the gravel beach they'd dropped anchor. "Better than perimeter guns...it can stay awake all night, and shoot anything that moves."

"I can do that, yes." Manny walked down the lowered gangway, aluminum food containers clasped within each claw. "That is, if I don't put myself in rest mode. Helps to conserve power, you know..."

"Shut up." Lars lay on the beach where he'd thrown down a thermal blanket, his back propped against the still-folded dome tent. He unwrapped a ration bar, carelessly tossing the wrapper into the cloverweed behind him. "When you get done unloading everything, you can set up the tent. Then you can get started on dinner." He glanced over at Marie. "What do you want to eat tonight?"

Before Marie could reply, Manny dropped the containers. "Mr. Thompson, I'll tell you this once, and once only. Appearances notwithstanding, I'm not a robot, and I refuse to be treated as such. If you want anything from me..."

"You're our guide, Robby. You volunteered for the job, remember?"

'A guide, not a slave...and as I was saying, if you want anything from me, then you'll treat me with common human respect. That begins with not calling me 'it' or 'Robby' or anything other than..."

"I dumped your metal ass in the river once." Lars stared at him. "Give me a reason to do it again...please."

Manny gave no answer. Instead, he strode across the beach to where Lars lay, until he was close enough for his shadow to fall across the young man. Lars hastily scrambled backward on his hands and hips, as if afraid that the savant was about to attack him. But Manny merely regarded him for a moment before he slowly turned his back upon Lars and, ever so deliberately, lowered himself to the ground, folding his legs together in lotus position. As Marie watched, the savant rested his hands upon his knees, lowered his head slightly, and became silent.

And there he remained for the rest of the afternoon and into the evening, motionless and quiet, even as daylight faded away and darkness came upon the tiny island.

Lars kicked at him, swore at him, even pulled out a rifle and threatened to shoot him. Yet Manny refused to budge; the multifaceted corona of his right eye, now dimmed ever so slightly, reflecting the setting sun a dozen different ways as he meditated upon whatever it was that savants thought about when they entered rest mode. By then it'd become obvious that they would receive no cooperation from him; Marie pitched the tent while Lars was still throwing his tantrum, and she finally managed to get him to help her gather driftwood for a campfire. Dinner came late, and was little more than sausage and beans warmed in a skillet above the fire; when they finished eating, Marie coaxed Lars into gathering the plates and utensils and washing them in the shallows. And still Manny remained inert and silent.

Bear was rising to the east, the leading edge of its ring-plane a spearhead against the gathering stars, when Marie lighted a fish-oil lamp and used it to illuminate the map she'd spread out on the ground next. "We've got to figure out where we're going," she said, kneeling over it. "We can't keep going down Sand Creek…"

"Why not?" Lars pointed to where it flowed into the East Channel. "Look, that's only a day away or so. Once we make the channel, all we have to do is follow it until we reach the big river." By that he meant the Great Equatorial River, which encircled Coyote like an endless, elongated ocean. "Get there, and we can go anywhere."

"Not the way we're going, we can't." Marie tapped a finger against the Eastern Divide, the long, high ridge that separated the New Florida inland from the East Channel.

"The only way through is the Shapiro Pass. Carlos went through that in a kayak, and it almost killed him."

"But we don't have a kayak. We've got that big mother over there…"

"Even worse." Marie let out his breath, looked up at him. "I've been through it, too, remember? In a keelboat, back in '03 when we evacuated Liberty. That was in mid-winter, when the water was high, and even then we nearly ripped out the bottom of the boat. The rapids… trust me, this time of year, the rapids are murder. We'll never make it."

"Yeah, yeah, okay." Lars had learned not to argue with Marie about the terrain of places where she'd already been. He pointed to the Garcia Narrows Bridge, northeast of their present location, where it crossed the East Channel to Midland from the Eastern Divide. "So we cut across country, take the bridge…"

"Can't do that either. That'll take us into Bridgeton and Forest Camp—" she indicated the settlements on the east and west sides of the bridge respectively "—and we were told to stay away from the other colonies."

"C'mon…you're not taking that seriously, are you?" A smirk came to his face. "I got friends in Bridgeton. Lester, Tiny, Biggs…I'm sure any of them would put us up for a few days." He gave her a wink. "Maybe even six months, if we play our cards right…"

"Or they would turn you in as soon as they saw you, and avoid jail time themselves."

Startled by the unexpected sound of Manny's voice, Marie looked up to see the savant gazing at them. Sometime during the last few minutes, he'd risen from his perch at the water's edge and turned to face them, a black specter half-visible by the firelight.

"No one will help you," Manny went on, as if he'd been part of the conversation all along. "The word is out, or at least it will be, by the time you make it to the next town. You're *persona non grata*. Bad company. Anyone who associates with you risks stockade time. I wouldn't count on...."

"I thought I told you to shut up." Lars scooped up an handful of gravel, flung it at the savant. It clattered off his metal chest, ineffective as it was impulsive; Manny didn't move, but simply stood there. Lars shook his head and looked down at the ground. "God, I need a drink. Didn't we bring any booze?"

"Did you ever stop to consider that drinking may be the source of all your...?"

"If you want to help," Marie said, "you can start by not lecturing us." Picking up the map, she stood up and walked over to him. "We need a place to go. If we can't go south or east, and north takes us back to Liberty..."

"Then it's obvious, isn't it? You should follow Horace Greeley's advice."

"Who the hell is Horace Greeley?" Lars muttered.

"'Go west, young man, go west.'" Taking the map from Marie, Manny studied it for a moment. She was surprised that he could see it without the aid of a flashlight, then remembered that he was gifted with infrared vision; bearlight was sufficient for his electronic eyes, even if one of them was permanently damaged. "If we cross Sand Creek and go west by southwest for about fifty miles, we'll arrive at the confluence of North Creek and Boid Creek. And if we follow Boid Creek upstream for another hundred and twenty miles, we'll reach the West Channel, just past the mouth of the Alabama River. From there…"

"Wait a sec." Marie held up a finger, then dashed back to the campfire to pull a pocket light from her pack. Bringing it back to where Manny stood, she switched it on and held it over the map so that she could read it as well. "Oh, no…no, that's no good. That's almost two hundred miles through back country, with the first fifty across dry land."

"The skimmer is designed for all-terrain travel. Deflate the pontoons, and it'll operate just as well in high grass. It'll run a little slower, granted, and we'd do well to avoid heavy brush, but once we reach Boid Creek, we'll make up for lost time."

"Aren't you forgetting something, Robby?" Still not rising from where he sat, Lars snapped a branch in half and fed it into the camp fire. "Back country means boid country. Maybe you don't have anything to worry about, but us flesh 'n blood types…"

"I have no more desire to encounter boids than you do, Mr. Thompson. I doubt they'd distinguish very much between a savant and a baseline human…and I've asked you not to call me Robby." He returned his attention to Marie. "The first fifty miles will be the toughest, I grant you that, but with luck and skillful driving we can probably travel the distance in only a day or two. Once we

reach Boid Creek, we'll be on water again. After we reinflate the pontoons, we should be able to cover…"

A harsh scream broke the quiet of the evening, a
high-pitched howl that drifted across the savannah and
caused the hair on the back of Marie's neck to stand. She
immediately switched off her light, even as Lars looked
around for where he'd left his rifle. Only Manny was un-
perturbed; pulling back the hood of his cloak, he turned
his head toward the direction from which the sound had
come, as if searching for its source.

"It's not close," he said. "No less than two miles, at
least. But…"

"But what?" Marie peered into the darkness. Once
again, she became just aware just how vulnerable they
were. The narrow creeks on either side of the island
offered little protection from what was out there.

"Wait," Manny said softly. "Just wait…." Then they
heard another boid cry, this time from a slightly different
direction, and a little louder than the first. "Ah, so," he
added. "That would be the mate. They work together,
frightening their prey into making them run first one way,
then another, until they become disoriented. Then…"

"I got the idea." Yet in all the years she'd spent on
Coyote, this was the first time she'd heard of this. Not
even Carlos, who had a boid skull on his cabin wall as a
hunting trophy, possessed that kind of insight. "So what
do we do?"

"Keep the fire going. They associate open flame with
brush fires caused by lightning storms, and they tend to
avoid those. Otherwise, all we need to do is stay where we

are and make as little sound as possible. We don't want to draw their attention." Folding the map, Manny handed it back to her, then walked over to the fire, where Lars crouched, rifle at hand. "Thank you for allowing me to recharge, Mr. Thompson. If you'll give me your weapon, I'll be happy to stand watch tonight."

Lars gazed at him warily, unwilling to surrender his carbine. "Give it to him," Marie said quietly. "He knows what he's doing...I think."

'Believe me," Manny said, "I do." Lars hesitated, then stood up and, without another word, relinquished the rifle to the savant. Manny checked the cartridge to make sure that it was fully loaded, then tucked it beneath his right arm, pulling back his robe so that it wouldn't get in the way. "Now go to bed, both of you. We have a long day ahead of us tomorrow."

"Yeah. Sure. Whatever." Standing a little straighter, Lars tried to muster what remained of his earlier bravado. "So what's for breakfast tomorrow, Robby?

"'I don't use it myself, sir...it promotes rust.'" Manny's voice became deeper and more mechanistic as he said this. It sounded like another quote, yet Marie couldn't quite put her finger on it. Humiliated, Lars slinked off to the tent, muttering something she didn't quite understand. She watched while he fumbled with the zipper, waited until he inside, then turned to Manny.

"Thanks, Savant Castro," she murmured. "I appreciate it."

"Of course, Ms. Montero." His voice returned to its former inflection. "And, by the way...my name's Manny."

She nodded, and began to walk away. Then she paused to look back to him. "I'm Marie," she said, as quietly as she could.

"Good night, Marie. Sleep well."

From the diary of
Marie Montero;
Uriel 49, c.y. 06

    Decided to start a diary today—this is my first entry. Found an old logbook in the bottom of the tool compartment while searching for something to help us clean grass from engine blades. Figure since we're going to be out on our own for awhile, might as well keep a record of where we've gone and what we've done. Got to report in every other day, so it'll help me keep track of stuff. Wendy's been keeping a journal for years, seems to help her put everything in perspective (is that the right word?), so maybe if I do the same thing it'll help me, too.

    Lars says I'm wasting time doing this, but I've got a lotta time to waste. Just spent last two days making our way across New Florida—seen nothing but grass, grass, and more grass. Trees now and then, but it's pretty much the same thing: miles and miles of grass, tall as my chest. Every ten miles or so we have to stop because the stuff gets caught in the fans and clogs them up, so when the engines start to overheat Lars pulls over and then Manny and I have to get out and yank all that grass out of the cowlings while Lars waits for the engines to cool down. But when we're not doing that, the only thing I have to do is sit there. Lars won't let me drive, and he doesn't like it when I talk to Manny. So it's pretty boring.

Manny's not such a bad guy, once you get to know him. We chit-chat while we clear the engines, and he's told me a bit about himself. Turns out that he was once a poet, back on Earth almost eighty-five years ago. Even wrote a couple of books. But he got some sort of disease that caused his bones to lose calcium and deteriorate, so when he got a chance to download his mind into a quantum comp and become a savant, he took it. Hearing this makes me think he's a little more human than I thought… but then I remember that he used to be the Matriarch's #2 man, and I try to keep this in mind before I trust him too much.

Spent last night (our second) somewhere in the savannah. Close as we can tell from looking at the map, we're about two-thirds of the way to where North Creek and Boid Creek come together. Lars wanted to push on until we got there, but Manny told him that it wouldn't be smart to travel at night. There's a lot of stuff out here— tree stumps, ball plants, even boid nests—that we could run into even with the floodlights on. Lars finally listened to him and stopped, but the grass was too high for us to make camp without doing a lot of clearing, so instead we stayed aboard, laying out our sleeping bags on the deck and eating cold rations for dinner.

Didn't sleep well. Kept hearing boids all night. Manny stood watch again—nice to have someone who doesn't need to sleep and who can see in the dark—but I woke up once when I heard something moving through the grass *pretty close to us. Looked up, saw Manny standing just a couple of feet from Lars and me. Bear was up high, so I could see him really well. He had his carbine raised to his shoulder and was aiming down at something I couldn't make out. He didn't fire, though, but just kept watching, and pretty soon I didn't hear the boid any more. Almost like it caught sight of Manny and decided not to mess with him.*

Lars missed the whole thing. Just kept snoring away. Took me awhile to shut my eyes again, though. When I woke up this morning, though, Manny didn't tell us what happened. He just gave us some cereal and sliced apples, and stood watch while Lars and I took turns to go off in the high grass to shit and pee. And then we were off again.

Made North Creek about 2 hours ago. Stopped to reinflate the pontoons, then hit the water and went south down it about five or six miles until we reached the junction of Boid Creek, where we turned W x NW and started heading toward West Channel. Feels good to be on the water again. Making good time now that we don't have to stop to clear the fans.

Will use the satphone later to call back home, tell Carlos what we've seen so far. Which ain't much. Stupid idea, sending us out here to explore the world. Ha! Just grass, grass, and more grass.

They were on the fourth day of the trip, little more than ten miles from the West Channel, when Marie was nearly killed.

As Manny promised, the journey became faster once the Armadillo reached Boid Creek and was on the water again. Although they were traveling against the current, it didn't slow the skimmer very much, so long as Lars kept the engines at full throttle and remained in the center of the creek. They camped overnight on a sand-bar just east of the confluence of the Alabama River, and the evening had passed uneventfully; once again, Manny stood watch while Lars and Marie slept in the tent.

The following morning, though, they awoke to find the sky overcast with iron-grey clouds. While the others had breakfast, Manny used the skimmer's comsat system to pull up a nowcast report from Liberty. Satellite images showed that a low-pressure front had rolled in from the west during the night, bringing with it a strong chance of storms. Back in the colonies, the change of weather wouldn't have mattered so much, but out here in the open…

"We should go as far as we can today," Manny said, "but we need to get off the water at the first sign of a thunderstorm."

"C'mon, what's a little rain?" Lars peered at him over the lip of his coffee mug. "You won't melt." Then he snickered. "Oh, wait, I forgot...you might draw lightning."

"If I happen to attract lightning, as unlikely as that may be, then you'll be the first to know. I sit behind you, remember?" Lars's smirk lapsed into a dark glower, and Manny went on. "It's not just lightning we have to worry about...if we get enough rain, we'll also have to worry flash-floods. If that happens, we'd rather be on dry land, don't you think?"

Despite himself, Lars had to admit that the savant had a point. Until the storms actually came, though, there was no reason why they shouldn't keep moving. So they put out their fire, struck camp, loaded their equipment back aboard the skimmer, and continued down the narrow river, with Marie and Lars taking turns on the middeck to watch for signs of bad weather.

Yet, although the air became cooler and a few drops of rain occasionally pattered against the canopy, the storm never arrived. The clouds became thick and heavy, and shortly after midday Marie spotted a blue-white lancet arcing between the sky and the ground. But the lightning strike was somewhere in the grasslands many miles to the south, so far away that, when the thunder finally arrived nearly a minute later, it was only a dull grumble. The front moved over and past them with little more than a vague threat of violence; by early afternoon, as they passed through the broad delta that marked mouth of the

Alabama River, the clouds were parted here and there to admit angular columns of pale yellow sunlight, ghostly stairways rising into the heavens.

Marie was in no mood to appreciate the sublime beauty of the moment; she had another problem to worry about. She didn't know whether it was anxiety or the diet of processed food—it had been two days since they'd had anything fresh to eat—but regardless of the reason, she'd come down with a case of diarrhea. Since the beginning of the trip, she'd learned to wait until they made rest stops along the way, but today her bowels refused to cooperate. The antacid tabs she'd found in the medkit didn't help much, and during the hours while Lars was running the engines hard in an effort to get out from under the storm, she hadn't dared to ask him to pull over so that she could make a quick dash into the tall grass.

Yet her guts had begun to cramp painfully, and unless she wanted to relieve herself over the middeck rail, she had to do something fast. So as soon as they were past the Alabama River, she demanded that Lars make an emergency landing. No, they couldn't wait until they reached the coast; she had to go, right now. Lars groused a bit, but one look at her face told him that she wasn't kidding. With a resigned shrug, he throttled down the engines and turned the Armadillo toward shore.

Marie was off the skimmer before Manny had a chance to lower the ramp. Scrambling down the ladder, she dropped into ankle-deep muck so thick that it threatened to pull her moccasins off her feet. Scowling as she grabbed at waterfruit vines for support, cursing with each bowlegged step she took, she clambered ashore, then scrambled up a muddy riverbank until she reached dry land. Then she plunged in the grass, searching for some place where she couldn't be seen from the skimmer.

A dozen yards from the creek, she found a spider-bush thicket high enough to afford her some privacy. Dropping her pants, she squatted behind it; relief was immediate and not a second too soon. Once she was done, she pulled up a handful of cloverweed and use it to clean herself, a trick she'd learned while in the Rigil Kent brigade. Then she stood up and bent over to pull her pants up from around her ankles.

It was when she raised her head again that she spotted the boid.

The giant avian stood less than twenty yards away, silently watching her from the tall grass within which it was concealed. So perfectly did its tawny feathers match the color of the sourgrass, she might have missed seeing it entirely if something hadn't moved near its feet. Perhaps it was a swamper or a creek cat, but it distracted the boid just enough that it moved its head ever so slightly to watch it go.

She caught a glimpse of its enormous beak, absurdly parrot-like yet large enough to decapitate her with a single bite, and involuntarily sucked in her breath. The sound she made was sufficient to draw the boid's attention; its head swiveled on its thick neck, and once again its black, button-like eyes fastened upon her.

Fighting the urge to run, Marie forced herself stare straight back at the creature. If it knew that it'd been seen, it wouldn't attack…or at least not immediately, because boids preferred to stalk their prey and catch them unaware. Yet now that it knew that it had been spotted, the attack would be inevitable. The short, spike-like plumage on the top of the boid's skull lifted—it was an adult male, as if that mattered much just now—and it rocked back and forth upon its legs, almost as if daring her to make a break for it.

Marie's mind raced, calculating her odds for survival. The distance between her and the boid was greater than the distance between her and the skimmer. Not much, but those few extra yards might make all the difference. If she ran fast as she could, she might be able to reach the creek before it caught her. But boids were fast; their legs were longer than her own, and they were accustomed to chasing down their prey and leaping upon them while they were…

Damn it! Too much thinking, and not enough action. "Aw, shit," she muttered, and then she turned and ran.

She might have had a good head-start, were it not for the spider-bush directly behind her. She'd forgotten about that. Swearing, she nearly charged headlong into it, and only barely managed to avoid being tangled within its thorny strands. Yet it cost her precious seconds; even as she dodged around the bush, she heard the boid screech, and knew without looking back that it was coming after her.

Air burned within her lungs as she raced for shore, her arms raised to swat aside the grass. The ground trembled slightly beneath her feet, and she instinctively knew that the boid had leaped over the thicket. Still, she refused to look back. The shore was close, very close;

already she could see the skimmer's aerial, protruding against light grey clouds tinted orange-red by the afternoon sun, so heart-achingly beautiful, and, in a moment of clarity, she realized it might be the last thing her eyes would ever see.

Oh god, oh god, oh god...oh dear lord, save me, I'll never do anything...oh god, please, I swear I'll...

A hot wind, stinking of decayed flesh, brushed against the back of her neck. A hard snap just behind her...

From somewhere to her left, the loud *poppa-poppa-poppa* of an automatic weapon, Looking around, she caught a glimpse Manny standing in the tall grass only a few yards away, hood thrown back, carbine raised to his shoulders.

"*Down!*" he yelled.

The gun's muzzle moved in her direction, and she dove headlong for cover. She hit the ground face-first, hard enough to knock the wind from her lungs. Rolling over, Marie saw the boid towering above her. For a second, she thought this was the end, then she heard gunfire again. The boid staggered backward, red blood and grey brains spurting from a hole in its head big enough for her to stick her hand. Gore spattered across her legs, then the creature toppled over, its taloned feet twitching as if, even in death, it was still trying to catch up with her.

Her mouth dry, her heart feeling as if it was about pound its way through her chest, Marie fell back against the trampled grass. A timeless time went by, then Manny loomed over her, a figure in black with a death's head for a face. He said something—it may have been *are you all right?* but she couldn't be sure, because his voice sounded scratchy and distant, as if it was a radio transmission from another world—and all she knew for certain was that she was drifting away to a dark, warm place, where there was no fear.

From the diary of
Marie Montero:
Uriel 52, c.y. 06 (extract)

When I came to, I was back aboard the skimmer. Manny [had] carried me back while Lars pulled anchor and started up the engines, so when I woke up, I found that we were already underway. Manny'd laid me out on deck and pulled the awning over me, and when I woke up, I found that he'd put a wet cloth across my forehead.

Very weird, coming out of it like that. Don't even remember fainting. In fact, that's a first for me—fainting, that is—but Manny says it's not unusual, considering how close I came to buying it. I asked him how close the boid was when he shot it and at first he wouldn't tell me, but when I told him about the snap I heard, he said that was the boid trying to bite my head off. That's how close it was.

Manny told me he'd come ashore when he saw that I'd gone off without a rifle. He had a hunch there might be trouble. Glad he had that hunch, or I would've been lunch, ha ha. Not funny, I know…but right now, laughing is a lot better than crying, and I've done some of that already.

Lars got us downriver a mile or two, then stopped engines and came back to see how I was doing. He was worried, too…at least I think he was…but then he went off on me about going ashore unarmed, and that I shouldn't ever take a dump again without packing a gun. Then he told Manny we should've hauled the boid aboard and carved it up for food, because we could've gotten a good meal out of it. I had to laugh at that. Hell, I was downright hysterical. Told him that it would've tasted even better if I'd fattened it up a little bit. That got him pissed off. He went back to the cockpit and started the engines again, and didn't say anything to me after I returned to the bubble.

Lars means well, I know that. And he was right about going ashore without carrying a rifle to protect myself. But, dammit, I was almost killed back there, and he's mad about not getting some fresh meat from the carcass?!

At any rate, we made it to the end of Boid Creek by the end of the day, where we found the entrance to the West Channel. So far as we know, we're the first ones to see the western side of New Florida. From here, it's about five miles across the channel to Great Dakota; we can see river bluffs on the other shore, with deep forests and high mountains that look almost black rising in the distance. Totally different landscape from New Florida—sort of like Midland, except even more rugged. What a relief. I'm so sick of sourgrass, I could puke.

It was too late for us to cross that night, so we made camp on New Florida, on the north side of the mouth of Boid River. For once, Manny made Lars haul everything ashore and set up the tents—he wanted to spend the last hour or two of daylight surveying the area (taking pictures, setting up the theodolite and making measurements, using a plumb-line to estimate the water depth, etc.). Says this place could be a good site for a port town, some time in the future. Guess I can see that, maybe...but Manny sees things a lot different from us, I think.

I made dinner, but it wasn't very good...burned the beans and undercooked the chicken (in fact, I couldn't even eat the chicken—reminded me too much of what almost ate me). Lars bitched about having to do all the hard work, but Manny stayed quiet. He spent the time writing up the report to send home—I asked him not to mention what happened today [because] I didn't want Carlos to get worried—and when he was done I read it over and let him transmit it. Then I crawled into the tent and tried to go to sleep.

Lars came in awhile later. Pulled off his clothes and made me take off mine. Wanted to have sex. Wasn't in the mood, but I let him, because he insisted. Felt good for about a minute, but I [crossed out]. It seemed to satisfy him, though, because after he was done he rolled over and fell asleep.

Needed to pee, so I moved him aside, crawled out of the tent. Found Manny standing by the fire, looking out over the channel. He wanted to escort me while I went into the bushes, but I told him I'd be OK. No boid cries—everything was calm and quiet. I didn't go far, just to the edge of the water, but I never let him out of my sight. He turned his back, but I could tell from the way he held his gun that he was on high alert.

When I was done he said goodnight and told me to have pleasant dreams. Before I went back to bed, I asked *him what he was doing, i.e. what did he do all night while Lars and I were sacked out.*

He said that he was writing poems.

Writing poems. I like that.

Although Marie, Lars, and Manny thought they were the first to navigate the southwest end of the West Channel, they soon learned they were wrong. Not long after the expedition crossed over from New Florida and began making its way down the east coast of Great Dakota, they unexpectedly came upon another group of explorers.

At Manny's insistence, Lars throttled down the engines and let the current carry them downstream. Although Lars was impatient to reach the Great Equatorial River, Manny wanted to take time to study the channel. When Marie agreed with the savant—after all, there was no reason for them to hurry—the pilot found himself outvoted. So while Lars fumed within the cockpit, Manny and Marie sat side by side on the middeck, legs dangling over the side, as they watched the river go by.

The day was pleasantly warm, with just a touch of autumn to the salt breeze wafting across the channel's dark blue expanse. Swoops circled above the faux-birch whose roots clung precariously to the edge of limestone bluffs rising above the river; now and then, channelmouth jumped from the water near the boat, as if frightened by the aliens who'd suddenly appeared in their midst. In the far distance, they could make out the highlands, enormous mountains so thickly forested with blackwood and rough bark that they looked like they were made of charcoal, save for the rocky summits that towered above the tree line.

Great Dakota was breathtakingly beautiful, as awesome in its unspoiled majesty as the savannahs of New Florida had been menacing. For the first time since they'd left Liberty, they were able to relax. There was no sourgrass to battle though, no boids to watch out for. After awhile, Marie and Manny stopped talking; instead they shared a quietude that was both respectful and intimate. Manny made notes in a datapad, but every so often he switched to the graphic-input function and used the tip of one of his claw-like fingers to render a quick sketch. Peering over his shoulder, Marie was surprised by the delicate lines he traced upon the screen. Manny was not only a poet, but also an artist; it was easy to forget that he was a savant, a soul locked within a mechanical body.

Around midday, Lars stopped the engines. He came up top to drop anchor, then stomped across the middeck to the stern where, without apology, he opened his fly and urinated into the river. Marie had taken off her shirt and now wore only her bra; looking around to catch Lars staring at her breasts, she found herself feeling naked, and quickly pulled her shirt on again before going below to make lunch.

Left alone with Manny, Lars leaned against an engine cowling; he crossed his arms and silently regarded the savant for a long time, idly scratching at his beard but never once saying a word. Manny put away his data pad and stood up to face the channel; he was better at practicing stoicism than Lars, and after awhile Lars turned and began plucking small blades of grass from the fans.

Marie came back up with sandwiches and some dried fruit; she and Lars ate in near silence, their only conversation some technical chatter regarding engine maintenance. Lars threw the rest of his sandwich overboard and watched a couple of channelmouth fight over it, then he stomped back across the deck, pulled up the anchor, and went back down the ladder.

Manny and Marie resumed their previous places on the deck. A few minutes later, the engines restarted and the skimmer began moving down the channel. Marie let out her breath, and for just a moment she heard the soft crackle from Manny's mouth grille that, in its own way, signified a sigh.

It was late in the afternoon when they spotted a thin tendril of smoke rising in the distance, from a point farther down the coast. At first Manny thought it was a forest fire caused by the storm that had passed over them the day before, but soon he and Marie realized that it was too small to be natural in origin. Lars must have thought so, too, for suddenly the engines suddenly revved up and both of them had to grab the railing as the skimmer rose higher upon its pontoons and began to cruise down the river.

They were right: the source of the smoke was a camp fire, set by people who'd already ventured down the West

Channel. As they grew closer, the bluffs gradually disappeared until they came within sight of a broad, flat delta where an inland creek emptied into the channel. A pair of keelboats lay at anchor just offshore, their sails furled. Nearby were several catskin tents, their poles leaning haphazardly as if carelessly planted in the muddy soil. And it was clear that they'd been spotted as well, for several figures stood on the sandy beach, waving their arms above their heads as the skimmer approached them.

"Who do you think they are?" Marie had climbed down the ladder into the cockpit; now she stood behind Lars, gazing at the camp site through the bubble.

"Does it matter?" Lars throttled back the engines as he turned the yoke toward shore. "First people we've seen in almost a week. Probably the only guys we're going to see this side of New Florida." He grinned. "Time to go over and say howdy."

"We're not supposed to make contact with anyone." Unnoticed by either of them, Manny had followed Marie belowdecks. "That's the condition of our..."

"Shut up, Robby." Lars shoved-down the throttle bars. The fans growled as the engines reverse-propped; the skimmer's bow rose slightly upon the crest of its own wake. "Ain't a colony, is it? So we can meet 'em if we want to." He glanced back at the savant. "And since when did you become boss?"

Marie kept her silence. Already, two men were wading out into the shallows, preparing to grab hold of the skimmer and help tow it ashore. Their beards were long and unkempt, their clothes ragged and patched together.

Upon the beach, several more men and women stared at them; although a couple held up their hands in greeting, she saw no welcoming smiles.

"He might be right," she murmured, feeling a forbidding chill. "Maybe we should…"

"Look, it's just for a little while, okay?" Lars cut the engines, let their momentum carry the skimmer the rest of the way ashore. "'Sides, we gotta make camp soon anyway. Why not with these guys?" He stared at her. "Anything wrong with that?"

"No…no, I guess not." Her voice was meek. "It's just that…"

"Yeah, well, hold that thought." Lars pushed himself out of his seat, then slid between her and Manny, practically shoving them out of the way in his haste to get topside. "Need to drop anchor before this heap drifts away."

Manny watched him as he scampered up the ladder. "Who knows?" he said quietly. "Maybe seeing someone else might do him some good."

Marie could already hear men clambering up the sides of the skimmer. Recalling stories of Caribbean pirates she'd heard when she was very young, it wasn't hard to visualize them with bandanas tied around their heads and daggers clenched within their teeth.

"Stay with me," she whispered. "Please, whatever you do…just stay with me."

From the diary of Marie Montero: Uriel 53, c.y. 05 (extract)

Stopping was a mistake. We should've stayed away, just waved and kept going. But Lars insisted, and Manny thought it might be good for him if he saw someone else besides just him and me. But if I could take it back, somehow run back the clock, we would've never set foot on the beach.

I was nervous about these people from the get-go, especially the way a couple of their guys climbed aboard without so much as a how-do. I didn't like the way they looked at me, like I was fresh meat they'd love to skewer. But Manny really put the spook on them...the last thing they expected to see was a Savant, not to mention one with a rifle in his hands, so they calmed down a bit once we came ashore, and introduced themselves as politely as they could.

Turns out they're a group from New Boston, about three hundred miles N x NE from where we found them. Twenty-seven in all, mostly men, although there's also a few women and a couple of children. They built the boats themselves and set out from Midland to explore the West Channel, mainly to see if they could find a location for a new settlement. They'd been on the river for about three weeks when we happened upon them, and they were just as surprised to see us as we were to see them.

That warned me right then and there that something was wrong. New Boston isn't a major colony, but it's well-off enough that no one ought to want to leave it to go exploring, or at least not in the last month of summer, with autumn just ahead. And these guys seem to have just enough to get by on...just a few patched-up tents and some hand-me-down equipment that's seen better days. Even their guns are old Union Guard flechette rifles left over from the war, and they didn't have but a few of those. Like they'd just grabbed whatever they could get their hands on before they shipped out.

But they've got plenty of booze. About six kegs of sourgrass ale, along with a few jugs of bearshine that they said they'd been saving for a special occasion. Soon as Lars heard that, I knew we were staying for the night, whether Manny or I liked it or not.

At least their leader is someone I can trust. Woman by the name of Chris Smith—guess it's short for Christine, although almost everyone calls her Missus Smith. Big lady, with arms that look like they could yank the wings off a boid. Real no-nonsense attitude. When one of the guys started to get a little frisky with me, she stepped in and stared him down. He backed off right quick, and after that the others decided to look but not touch. At least for awhile.

They got a bonfire started shortly after sunset, and a couple of guys fried some redfish they caught this morning. For awhile, it wasn't so bad: just a bunch of people, chowing down around the camp fire and swapping stories about what we've seen and done since we left home. Lars didn't tell anyone exactly why we'd left Liberty, and none of them told us exactly why they'd left New Boston, but after awhile I got the feeling that the reasons were pretty much the same. These people were too ornery for the place where they'd come from, and someone had told them to hit the road and not come back.

Well, good enough. But then a few of the men got into serious drinking, and that was when I noticed that the rest, including all the women and children, began making themselves scarce. The only woman who stayed behind was Missus Smith. She parked herself on a log next to me, and I noticed that her right hand never strayed far from the big hunting knife she kept in a scabbard on her belt.

Manny was there, too. Although no one liked having him around—all through dinner, he had to put up with stuff like "Hey, where'd you get you get the pet robot?" and "Maybe we can break him down for spare parts"—he never left my side, and stood behind me while we ate. He said nothing, and after awhile people pretty much forgot he was there.

So it was Manny and Missus Smith who saved me from getting gang-raped, because I have no doubt that's what would've happened if they hadn't been there. I was getting tired, and about ready to head for our tent, when Lars happened to remark that we hadn't brought any liquor of our own, and would anyone consider making a trade for a jug of bearshine.

Someone suggested that they'd swap a jug for one of our carbines, but Lars shook his head and told him that we only had two and we needed both of them. Another guy said that he'd settle for our satphone, and for a moment I thought Lars would actually do that, so I said that we needed it, too, no thanks. And then someone else—a skinny guy named James—said that he'd trade up for a night with me.

Lars looked at him. Then he looked at me. Then he looked at the jug James was holding out. And then he just shrugged and said, "Sure, why not?"

At first I thought he was joking. I mean, there was a smile on his face when he said this. But then James said, "All right, it's a deal" and then he stood up and started toward me. "Let's go, honey-doll. We got a big night ahead of us."

That's when I knew he wasn't kidding. He meant to drag me off to his tent and...well, you can guess the rest. And not only that, but since his pals stood up as well, it was pretty clear that James wouldn't mind having company. Lars did nothing to stop them, though. James handed him the jug, and Lars pulled out the cork and treated himself to a big swig of corn liquor. Didn't even look at me.

Chris stood up and pulled out her knife. "No deal," she said. "Everyone just stay put and no one gets hurt." But they didn't back down. After all, she was outnumbered at least six to one. No matter how tough she might be, there's no way she could take them all at once.

Then there was a shot behind us, and I knew without looking that Manny had fired his gun in the air. Everyone jumped except for Lars, who just stayed where he was, cool as can be, while Manny lowered the gun and pointed it straight at James.

No one said a word, but James and his posse backed off. They went back to where they'd been sitting, and for a couple of minutes no one said anything. Then someone remarked that Bear had come up and didn't it look pretty tonight, and pretty soon everyone was back to talking about the weather and fishing and what-else, as if nothing had happened.

Chris didn't sit down, though, and she didn't put her knife away. She nudged me with her elbow and cocked her head toward the skimmer. That was all the advice I needed. I stood up and, with Manny beside me, walked back to where we'd beached the skimmer. I didn't breathe easy until I'd climbed back aboard, and didn't feel safe until I went belowdecks.

I'm sleeping in the skimmer tonight, with the hatch shut and Manny standing watch topside, as he'd done while we still on New Florida. It's not boids he's on the lookout for, though, but James and his buddies. Lars hasn't returned and I hope he doesn't. Looking through the cockpit at the bonfire, I can hear him: laughing, singing, getting drunk. Not a care in the world.

Sure know how to pick 'em, don't I?

ars seemed to remember nothing of what had happened the night before. When Marie saw him again the following morning, his clothes were grimy from having slept on the beach next to the bonfire. His breath reeked of alcohol, and he claimed to have no recollection of attempting to trade her for a jug of bearshine. So far as he was concerned, all he'd done was have a little party with some newfound friends. But Marie couldn't help but notice that he was unable to look her in the eye, or that he avoided having anything to do with Manny.

She wanted to leave at once, as did Manny. While Lars stumbled off toward the latrine, the two of them packed up their gear. Much to her surprise, nothing appeared to be missing; the fact that they'd left most of their equipment aboard the skimmer probably had something to do with this. The half-dozen men who'd stayed up all night were still sleeping off their hangovers; those who were awake studiously avoided Marie and Manny while they disassembled the tent and rolled up the sleeping bags, yet just as they were about to carry everything to the skimmer, Chris Smith came over to them.

"Just wanted to say I'm sorry about what happened last night." Like Lars, she had trouble looking at Marie, and instead gazed at the smoldering remains of the bonfire. "What James said and did was…" Her voice trailed off, and she shook her head. "Look, it's no way to treat a guest, let's put it that way."

"No, it wasn't." Marie was tempted to turn her back on Missus Smith until she saw how embarrassed the woman was. "Appreciate you standing up for me," she added, her tone softening. "Would've been worse if you hadn't."

"Yeah, well…" Straightening her broad shoulders, she turned to look at the nearby tents. "My fault. James and his boys seem to think they run the show here. They tried this once before with some of the other women. I put it down then, thought it wouldn't happen again. If I'd known it would, I would've warned you." She hesitated. "Besides, I thought your man would've…I mean, that he would have defended you, not…"

"You're no more surprised than I am." Marie turned to look in the direction Lars had gone. Through the brush that marked the edge of the camp site, she saw him standing at the edge of the latrine pit, his back turned to them as relieved his bladder. As she watched, he abruptly collapsed to his hands and knees; even from the distance, she could hear gagging sounds as everything in his stomach forced its way up through his throat. No longer did he resemble the guerrilla fighter with whom she'd fallen in love, but instead a pathetic drunk. All of a sudden, she realized how much she had come to despise him.

"If I could leave him behind," she murmured, "I'd do so in a heartbeat."

Chris quietly regarded her a moment. "Got a minute?" she asked at last. "Or are you in a hurry to get out of here?" Marie looked back at her, and Missus Smith nodded toward the water's edge. "Take a walk with me, sister. I got a proposition for you."

Marie glanced at Manny. The savant nodded, then reached forward to take the folded tent from her. As Manny carried their equipment to the skimmer, Chris led Marie down the beach, away from the camp site.

"You probably figured out by now that we're not your usual settlers," Chris said once they were out of earshot of anyone else. "Fact is, most of us are here 'cause we got fed up with New Boston. It's become an iron town ever since they found the Gillis lode, and these people aren't the kind who want to spend their lives down in some mine with pick-axes in their hands. So we gathered up what little we could and sailed off down the channel, looking for some place to start our own colony."

"Makes sense. We've had people like that leave Liberty since the war was over."

"I know. I was in Forest Camp during the occupation, working on the bridge project. So's most everyone else here. When Rigil Kent blew up the bridge, we headed north and started New Boston. So we're used to cutting timber, not digging holes. But..." She shrugged. "Well, lately I've begun to wonder just how serious some of these guys really are."

"I don't understand."

Missus Smith stopped and turned toward the beach. "Take a look around, tell me what you see." Without waiting for her to respond, she pointed inland. "I'll tell you what I see. Plenty of dry land past the beach, with a freshwater river leading down from the mountains. No boids to worry about...they're all on the other side of the channel. And up there in the hills, all the wood you could possibly want. Good, solid timber, too...not just black-wood and faux-birch like on New Florida, but rough bark and mountain briar as well. With some work, this place could become a major settlement."

In her mind's eye, Marie perceived the place as Chris imagined it: not as a broken-down fishing camp, but as a thriving frontier colony. And she had a point. Most of Liberty, and much of Midland on the other side of the Eastern Channel, had already been deforested during the Union effort to build the Garcia Narrows Bridge. Although this place was farther away from Liberty than Forest Camp, she'd already glimpsed the vast, untouched wilderness of Great Dakota. There was potential here, no doubt about it.

"Have you talked about this with anyone else?" she asked.

Missus Smith let out her breath as a dry snort. "Sure I have. We've been here nearly two weeks, y'know. And a few of us see it as I do. But James and his bunch..." She absently kicked a clump of beach grass in frustration. "Should've never let them get into the booze. Hell, if I'd known they'd turn into a bunch of drunks, I'd never let 'em bring it in the first place. Now all they want to do is drink and fish, and half the time they're too messed up to fish. Like this is a vacation or something."

She looked at Marie. "Last night was the last straw," she went on, more quietly now. "I've had it with 'em. No more parties, no more trying to gang-bang anyone with tits. So I'm cutting 'em loose."

Marie stared at her. "You can do that?"

"Sure, I can." A grim smile. "Second day out from New Boston, when we made camp on the north shore of New Florida, James and I had a little disagreement about who was in charge. So we had an election, winner take all. I won. And believe me, I can make it stick. Maybe you didn't see it last night, but there's a lot of people among us who are just as sick and tired of him and his pals as I am." Missus Smith patted the knife on her hip for effect. "If I tell em to go, then they'll go."

"Sure, but...where'd they go?"

"I don't care." She pointed to the two keelboats anchored near the skimmer. "They can take either one of the boats...both are in good condition. Load up their tents and take the booze with 'em, and head any which way they choose. North, east, west, south...wherever they can get the news. So long as they're not hanging around here, causing trouble."

She paused. "If you want to get rid of your man," she said, very quietly, "here's your chance. I saw what he tried to do last night. He would've pimped your ass for a jug of bearshine. Whatever caused you to light out for the country with him is none of my business, but..."

"I know." Marie looked back at camp. Lars was nowhere to be seen, yet she felt his presence nonetheless, and it gave her a chill. Sometime in the last week, the tough-minded yet easy-going guy whom she'd met during the Revolution had disappeared. Perhaps he'd never been there in the first place; all she'd seen was what she had wanted to see. Yet the fact remained that, from the moment they'd left Liberty, all he'd given her was heartache and misery. Two days ago, he'd shown no remorse when she'd been attacked by a boid. And last night...

"Can Manny stay?' she asked abruptly.

"The savant?" Chris thought about it for a moment, then shrugged. "I'm not crazy about those kind, but if you really insist..."

"I mean it. If I stay, he stays, too." She hesitated. "Look, he saved my life. Twice now, in fact."

"Yeah, yeah, all right." Missus Smith smiled. "He's handy with a gun, I've give him that much." Then her smile faded, and her expression became more serious. "So, are you with us? Or do you want to take your chances with Lars? Tell me now, because I need to know where you stand."

Marie took a deep breath. "I'm with you."

"Good." Missus Smith clapped her on the shoulder. "Glad to have you with us. Now let's go and read 'em the riot act."

Lars didn't take Marie seriously at first. Even when she climbed aboard the skimmer to throw his belongings on the beach, he seemed to think she was simply having a fit; he stood nearby with his arms crossed, a knowing smirk on his face. It was not until Missus Smith told him to pick up his gear and carry it to the closer of the two keelboats that he realized this wasn't a joke. He was being expelled, along with the New Boston colonists who'd been at last night's drinking party.

His disbelief quickly turned to anger, as did everyone else's being forced to leave. Yet Missus Smith had the upper hand; she'd already spread the word to all those in camp who were tired of being bullied by James and his cronies, and they'd decided the time had come to stand up for themselves. They'd showed up with guns, machetes, tree branches, anything that could be used as a weapon. Seeing that he and his pals were outnumbered, James tried to bargain with her, making promises that they'd behave from now on, but Missus Smith remained firm. James's group would be given one of the boats and a fair share of the supplies, including a couple of flechette rifles and a satphone in case of an emergency. They could take the rest of the ale and bearshine, too. Yet there was no question that they were being sent their own way, or that Lars was going with them.

Lars became ugly. Red-faced, stamping at the ground like a petulant child, he heaped foul words upon Marie, calling her things that, until now, she'd never imagined that he could think about her. Perhaps it was only the heat of the moment, but it was then that she realized for the first time that he'd never really loved her; she'd been little more than a toy he'd found, useful for sex and little else. Truth be told, she'd felt much the same way about him, too; the events of the past several days, though, had shown her that Lars was only a mannish boy who thought of no one but himself.

Nonetheless, his last words to her stung the most. "You can't get along without me," he said as he bent down to pick up his sleeping bag. "You know it, too."

"Yes, I can." She fought to keep her expression stolid, yet tears welled in the corners of her eyes. "I don't need you."

"Yeah, you do. You'd be dead by now if it wasn't for me." He looked past her toward Manny. The savant stood a few yards away, carbine in his hands. "Who you gonna depend on now, that thing? Hell, it ain't nothing more'n a two-legged can opener."

"He saved my life. And he didn't try to trade me for a jug of booze. More than I can say for you."

"No?" Lars slung the pack over his shoulder, tucked the bag under his arm. "Let's see him keep you warm at night, then." An ill-humored grin split his face. "Hell, I'd pay good money to see that. Might be as much fun as watching you and James..."

She stepped forward and slapped him across the face. The blow was harder than she meant it to be; that, or he simply didn't see it coming. Either way, he staggered back, almost tripping over his own feet as the sleeping bag fell from his arms. His eyes were wide with astonishment, his cheek reddened where she'd struck him; although his mouth opened, for a moment he was speechless.

Behind him, a couple of men from James' group snickered. Someone muttered something that Marie didn't catch, but Lars apparently did. The swollen corner of his upper lip curled, and Lars started toward her, dark fury in his eyes.

"That's enough," Missus Smith said. Hearing a low click to her left, Marie looked around. She'd raised her rifle and was pointing it straight at Lars. "Any closer, and so help me I'll put an end to you."

"Chris...."

"Hush." Missus Smith didn't look away from Lars. "No more words. You're done here. Pick up your stuff and get on the boat. Now."

Lars said nothing. He leaned over to retrieve his sleeping bag, now laying unrolled upon the sand like a dead worm. For a moment, Marie thought he'd mutter a curse or a last threat, yet Lars surprised her by remaining silent. Instead, he quietly slung the bag over his shoulder, turned away from them and marched down the beach to the keelboat.

James was waiting for him. The two men spoke for a few seconds, then James swatted him on the shoulder and let Lars climb aboard. Two other men shoved the boat backward into the surf, then were hauled over the side by their companions. The morning tide pulled the craft out into the channel, and the people on shore watched as the seven outcasts hoisted sails and tacked into the wind. Within minutes, they were gone, sailing southwest toward the Great Equatorial River.

"Good riddance," Missus Smith said quietly. "With any luck, we've seen the last of 'em."

Marie raised a hand to wipe away the tears sliding down her face. For the first time since they'd met, she was free of Lars. And yet, despite all reason not to do so, she knew they'd meet again.

**From the journals of
Wendy Gunther:
Uriel 54, c.y. 06**

*We heard from Marie today—not a mission report,
but a real-time call via satphone. I was on duty at the
hospital, but Carlos was home when she called. He spoke
with her, and told me about it once I got home. By then
he'd calmed down a little, but the conversation clearly
upset him.*

*In short: Marie has left Lars. Or rather, she's made
him leave her. She told Carlos that Lars had become abu-
sive since they left Liberty, to the point that he'd almost
allowed her to get killed a few days ago—a run-in with
a boid that, for some reason, she hadn't mentioned in
her last report. It seems that matters came to a head two
nights ago after they crossed the West Channel, when they
met up with a group from New Boston who'd made camp
on Great Dakota. Apparently some of these people were
rather...well, unpleasant, to put it mildly...but they had
plenty of liquor, and Lars went on a binge with them.*

*Carlos says that his sister wasn't very specific about
what occurred next, but apparently something happened
that gave her reason to become afraid of what might
occur if Lars remained with her. Whatever it was, it must*

have been pretty bad, because Carlos said Marie broke down while she was talking to him. And that was enough for her, and for the rest of the people in the camp; the next morning, their leader told the troublemakers to get lost, and to take Lars with them.

So Lars is gone, and Marie and Manny have elected to stay for awhile on Great Dakota, helping the rest of the group establish a new settlement. Although Carlos is relieved that Marie hasn't been hurt and that she's no longer with Lars—so am I; neither of us ever liked him very much—he's also angry that she's broken the conditions of her parole, i.e. that she and Lars were to explore as much of Coyote as they could during the next six months, and to avoid contact with any other colonists. On the other hand, realistically speaking, there's not much we can do to stop her, short of sending a couple of blueshirts out in a gyro to pick her up and bring her home. And what good would that accomplish?

We've discussed the situation with the magistrates, and come to agree that, at least for the time being, we just should wait and see what happens. If Marie and Manny have located a prime location for a new colony—and from what she's told Carlos, Great Dakota could become a major timber resource—then it's probably best that they explore it with others. After all, they're the first people to cross the West Channel; the other side is wilderness no one else has seen before. So it makes no sense for them to go at this alone when they've found other people who share the same objectives.

As for Lars...well, that was a tough call. One of the rules we'd set out was that they were to stay together, with Manny as their guide. Marie broke that rule when she allowed the New Boston group to expel him. We've talked this over with Clark Thompson. As much as he loves his nephew, he and Molly are aware of Lars' problems—especially his drinking—and he knows how much trouble he can cause. On the other hand, he's upset that Marie allowed him to be cut loose. He thinks Manny had something to do with this, even though Carlos told him that this was apparently Marie's decision, and he seems to believe that Lars should have been allowed to stay. But again, he knows there's not much he can do about it, so all he can do is hope that Lars will reappear sooner or later, and that by then Marie will have forgiven him for whatever he did.

Carlos is worried sick about his little sister. Maybe she's not so little any more, but nonetheless he remembers when they were kids and he always had to look out for her. He's felt responsible for her ever since their folks were killed a few days after we arrived on Coyote and the two of them became orphans (I had the same problem, of course, but since I didn't know my father very well, the situation was different for me). When I got home, I found him gathering his outback gear. He planned to enlist a gyro pilot to fly him out west so he could track down Marie. I talked him out of it, but he's still pacing the floor.

So now Marie is on her own, or at least without Lars. Well, maybe that's the way it was meant to be. But there's one thing that still puzzles me. In her reports, she seldom mentions Manny. Wonder why that is?

With the camp's population reduced by one-fourth, the first days without those seven men were the hardest. Although several weeks remained before the autumn equinox, it was clear that Coyote's long summer was drawing to a close; the days were beginning to get cooler, the nights a little longer. If the twenty-two remaining men, women, and children—who now included Marie and Manny—wished to settle Great Dakota, they would have to prepare for the hard, cold months that lay ahead. Cabins needed to be built, along with outhouses, storage sheds, and a greenhouse; autumn crops had to be planted, firewood cut and stockpiled: those and a dozen other tasks that James and his crew, who'd been among the hardiest of the original group, had ignored in favor of drinking and sport fishing.

Now that they were gone, though, there was nothing left to distract the others from the serious business of homesteading. Two nights after Lars left, Missus Smith called to order a town meeting, held after dinner around the community fire pit. After it was decided that the settlement would incorporate itself as Riverport, pending approval of the Colonial Council, an election was held for the town mayor. To no one's surprise, Missus Smith ran unopposed.

When Chris presented a motion formally inviting Marie and Manny to become town members, Marie was stunned to find the vote was unanimous in their favor. Perhaps she'd been an outcast in Liberty, but in Riverport she was a fellow citizen. Nor did anyone make an issue of the fact that Manuel Castro was a savant, even though almost everyone was aware that he'd once been the lieutenant governor of the New Florida colonies during the Union occupation. All the same Marie was struck by the irony that Riverport's mayor shared her first name with Liberty's Chief Proctor: one had welcomed her with open arms, while the other had thrown her in the county jail.

"You two aren't the only ones with a past," Chris said to her after the meeting was over. "Everyone here's running from something." Then she smiled and patted her on the shoulder. "Look you've got a clean slate. Whatever you or Manny did is over and done. So forget about it, okay? Time to start fresh."

And so she did. Over the course of next several weeks, Marie joined the effort to transform Riverport from a squalid collection of tents into something that resembled a frontier settlement. It was hard work, relentless and seldom pleasant. Once the camp was relocated from the beach to higher ground beside the nearby river, an adjacent stand of faux-birch was designated as timber for the construction of permanent structures. Her first task of the day usually involved helping the men cut down trees, strip them of branches, then lash ropes around the trunks and drag them to where cabins would be built. After lunch, she'd help the women and children clear a nearby meadow for the crops that would eventually be planted. And if there was any time left in the day, she collected firewood, washed clothes, cleaned fish, did some of the cooking, and whatever else needed to be done.

Although Manny wasn't strong enough to offer much assistance in the more grueling chores—despite appearances, his mechanical body wasn't meant for hard labor—he proved to be an able architect and civil engineer, designing not only cabins, but also viaducts and sewage systems. He performed water-table measurements that accurately predicted the locations for artesian wells, and once he learned less physically demanding crafts such as carpentry and fishing, he turned out to be adept at them as well. Logs shaved and trimmed beneath his tireless hands had precise fittings; the trotlines he rigged every morning produced enough channelmouth, redfish, and brownhead to feed everyone by day's end.

For the first couple of weeks, Marie and Manny saw little of each other. She shared a tent with another woman whose former companion had been among those who'd been expelled, while Manny stayed aboard the skimmer. Although it had been beached, he made sure that its engines remained in proper operating condition. Their work schedules seldom coincided; when she was with the timber crew, he was helping build cabins, and when she was planting seed for corn, wheat, and radishes, he cut bait for the trotlines. Yet as time went on and they became accustomed to their duties, the two found opportunities to talk.

As before, when they'd been on the river, Marie found herself amazed by his insights. Even with only one functional eye, little escaped Manny's notice. The seasonal migration of sea-swoops toward their breeding grounds in the distant Meridian Archipelago; day by day, he counted their numbers, taking note of how many birds were in each flock that passed overhead, and how that indicated the coming of autumn. The gradual changes in the night sky, the way bright stars like Acturus and Canopus seemed to rise a little earlier every evening. One afternoon they witnessed a solar eclipse, when Bear passed between Coyote and 47 Ursae Majoris; it happened often enough that Marie had long-since become accustomed to them, but Manny pointed something out to her that she'd never really noticed before, the way the winds rose from the east at the beginning of the eclipse, abruptly died off during totality, then rose again from the west during the end. Just one more thing she'd taken for granted, yet which fascinated him.

Indeed, Manny was everything that Lars hadn't been. He was always gentle, never raising his voice to her, and although he was gifted with vastly superior intelligence, not once did he ever condescend to her. She found solace in his presence, and found herself longing for his company when he wasn't around. In time she forgot almost entirely about Lars, except to occasionally wonder what he'd do once his pals ran out of booze, and whether that meant he'd reappear to make her life miserable again.

Lars's departure had one unforeseen side-effect. Although Missus Smith used the skimmer's satphone to transmit a formal petition to the Colonial Council for ratification of Riverport as a colony, the motion failed in the executive committee by a vote of 4-3. When Marie asked why this happened, Carlos told her that the dissenting vote had come from Clark Thompson. Lars's uncle was still angry about his nephew's expulsion. In his capacity as a influential committee member, he didn't want to do anything that might result in vital materials being shipped to the fledgling settlement. So until Lars reappeared, if ever, Riverport was nothing more than a squatter camp unrecognized by the Coyote Federation. Petty politics, really, but the only alternative was to make contact with James's group and beg them to return. Chris was firmly opposed to that idea, and so was Marie.

Yet even that was little more than a nuisance. Once the crops were planted, Marie found more opportunities to spend time with Manny. By then he was beginning to survey the nearby forests. In her desire to find reasons for the Council to recognize Riverport, Missus Smith wanted to make a case for Riverport becoming a major source of timber for all the colonies, and she'd put Manny in charge of scouting out the nearby woodlands. So Marie and Manny would follow the river upstream into the foothills, then hike upward through dense forests of rough bark and swoop's nest briar until they reached a granite bluff upon a steep ridge overlooking town. This lonely spot on Thunder Ridge became a favorite place for them to rest—although Manny didn't really need to do, he never forgot that she wasn't a savant—and compare notes on what they'd found.

The fifth day of Adnachiel was surprisingly warm, at least for the first week of autumn. Behind them rose the rocky summits of the Black Mountains, forbidding in their stark majesty. A few miles to the east lay the broad expanse of the West Channel, bright sunlight sparkling upon its cool blue waters. Manny sat cross-legged upon the bluff, sketching the view upon his pad. Marie lay on her side, quietly observing the delicate way his forefinger traced the river upon the pad's opaque plate.

A notion occurred to her, and she reached forward to tap his arm. "Hey, do you ever draw people?"

His head swiveled toward her. He'd pulled back the his robe's cowl, so she saw his face clearly. Although it remained expressionless, there was something in the way that he tilted his head that caused her to imagine a wry grin. "On occasion," he replied. "No one has ever posed for me, though, so I have to do it when they're not looking."

"I'll pose." She smiled. "I'd love to have a picture of me."

The metallic buzz from his mouth grill that she'd come to recognize as laughter. "Certainly. It'd be my honor." He shifted around so that he faced her, propping his pad on one raised knee. "How would you like to...?"

"I'll show you." Grasping the bottom of her shirt, she pulled it over her head in one swift motion. She reached behind her back and unsnapped her bra. Tossing it aside, she shook out her hair, then stretched out upon the granite, feeling its cool, gritty texture against her skin.

"Like this," she said, her voice soft and low.

Manny stared at her, his right hand poised above the pad, He said nothing for a few moments, then he lowered his head. "Please put your shirt back on."

"It's all right." Marie gave him a shy smile. "No one

can see me but you." She paused. "I don't want anyone but you to see me."

Manny put the pad aside, and said nothing for a few seconds. "Whatever it is you want from me," he said at last, "I can't give it to you."

"You already have. You're my friend..."

"Then be my friend, and..." He stopped, slowly raising his head. "Marie, have you ever wondered why I became a savant? Why I chose to have my mind scanned, downloaded into *this?*"

Raising his right claw, he tapped it against his chest, where his quantum comp lay. A dull, metallic clank, like a fork rattling against an empty skillet. "Because I was ill. In fact, I was ill all my life. The only part of me that was healthy was my brain. The rest...I spent my life in a wheelchair, with a respirator tube running up my nose and a nurse pushing me around."

"Manny..."

"Just listen, please." The afternoon sun reflected off the ruby orb of his left eye, turning it into a jewel. "I never walked on my own. I never ran, or played games with other children, or did anything that I couldn't do with my hands. Or at least my right hand...the left never worked very well." He paused. "And, no, I've never been with a woman, if that's what you're thinking."

Suddenly, the day felt cold, as if summer had abruptly come to an end. "I'm sorry," she said, sitting and reaching for her shirt. "I didn't mean to..."

"No, of course you didn't." He shook his head. "I know all about cruelty, and that wasn't your intent." Again, the short buzz. "Misplaced flirtation, perhaps, but not cruelty. But seeing you this way...well, the gesture is appreciated, but it's also one of those things I've tried not to think about."

Marie slowly nodded. Neglecting her bra, she hastily pulled the shirt over her head. "Please forgive me. I just..." She sighed, looked away. "Hell, I don't know what I was thinking."

"I know. Just an impulse." Then he hesitated, a little longer this time. "One thing, though...something I noticed when you were...shall we say, disrobed?"

She laughed at the diplomatic way he chose his words. "You mean when I was half-naked and trying to play sex kitten?"

"If you wish." Another pause. "It wasn't until you took off your shirt that I was certain of something I've observed before. Your breasts have become larger."

Marie stared at him. As busy as she'd been over the past several weeks, she hadn't been paying close attention to herself. Now that he mentioned it, though, she realized that her brassieres had become a bit uncomfortable lately. And although she'd eaten as well as anyone in camp could, given the fact that they were living on a diet of fish, waterfruit, rice, and beans, there were mornings when she'd been unable to keep anything in her stomach.

"Oh, god," she murmured. "Don't tell me what I think you're telling me."

"I'm not telling you anything. Only let me ask a personal question." He hesitated. "When was the last time you had your period?"

**From the diary of
Marie Montero:
Adnachiel 5, c.y. 06**

I'm pregnant.

Yeah, I'm sure. Found a test stick in the med kit. Peed on it, watched it turn red. You know the saying: stick turns green, a virgin you've been, stick turns red, you've been naughty in bed. Ha-ha. Not so funny now.

Looking back, I think I've known for awhile, but was trying not to admit it to myself. All the signs were there: morning sickness, cold sweats, craving for fish and sweets, tits getting bigger and more sensitive. And, of course, that period I missed a couple of weeks ago. But it took Manny to make me see what I didn't want to see.

Don't know how I could've been so stupid. We brought pills, of course—they were in the med kit, too— but for some reason I forgot to take them. Maybe it was because I wasn't having sex with Lars. But that night when he forced himself on me...well, that must have done the trick. So now I'm knocked up, and...

[Passage deleted]

Don't know how to feel about this. Angry at Lars for getting me in this position (or any other position, ha-ha—sorry, another bad joke) but also at myself for being so careless. But also scared. Last thing I need right now is worrying about having a baby.

Manny and I talked it over tonight, aboard the skimmer where we wouldn't be overheard. He let me have a good cry and once I got it out of my system he gave me a cloth to dry my tears. Then we discussed what I should do.

He figures that I'm about four or five weeks pregnant. Means I'll be due in about two and a half months Coyote-time. So I should expect to have the baby by the end of the year, sometime between Hanael 45 and New Year's Day.

Abortion out of the question. Even if I wanted to do that...and I don't, 'cuz it's against my principles...there's no one here to perform the procedure. Not safely, at least, and I refuse to let anyone get near me who doesn't know what they're doing. And even tho' the med kit has pregnancy strips and contraceptive pills, for some dumb reason there's no whoops-silly-me pills.

Leaves me with two choices. Stay here in Riverport, and have the baby in a town that's going to have a rough time getting through winter as is without having one more mouth to feed, or pack up and head back to Liberty where there's a half-decent clinic and a sister-in-law who's used to delivering babies.

Might think the choice is obvious, but it's not. For one thing, I'm still in exile. If I go back, I'd have to fill out my sentence. That means the baby gets born in jail, with Mama going off to the road crew every morning, Even if the maggies cut me some slack, I'll still go back to being the bad apple no one wants around, not even my own brother. Just some stupid girl who got preggers and had to crawl home with a baby in her belly, looking for mercy and hoping that someone would take her in. If I'm lucky, someone will take pity on me and give me a job washing dishes or something.

But here, I'm a respected member of the community. No one cares what I once was or what I once did 'cuz just about everyone else here has something in their past, too. Sometimes it seems like we're just getting by, but today we finished putting a roof on another cabin. Even if it leaks, it's a place someone can live, not just some crappy tent. That means something…and dammit, I like having a life that means something!

I want my child to grow up the same way.

Manny says I don't have to rush into this. The pregnancy is still early, so I've got some time to decide what to do. We're not telling Chris or anyone else what's going on until I figure things out. Hope she'll forgive me, but I'm not ready to pop the news just yet.

I'm scared. Goddamn, but I'm scared. Least I don't have Lars around, though, Sure, he's the other half of this problem, but I remember what he did to me and I don't want him being the father of my child.

Where is he, anyway?

Two days later, they heard from Lars again.

The satphone transmission might have been missed if Manny hadn't been aboard the skimmer, using its side-looking radar to verify the topographical estimates of the maps he and Marie had made. Considering that it was one of those rare occasions when he switched on the instrument panel for anything besides a quick system check-up, it was pure luck that Lars' satphone call was intercepted. Yet as soon as Manny heard a familiar voice coming through the transceiver— *"Mayday, mayday, is anyone there?"*—he reached over to pick up the hand mike.

Marie was helping raise a cabin's roof beam when one of the kids raced into town from the beach, breathlessly telling her that Mr. Castro needed to see her right away. She might have waited until the beam was safely hoisted into place if the child hadn't added that Manny had just heard from Lars, and that it was an emergency. Someone quickly stepped in to take her place at the pulley-rope, and she jogged across Riverport to the beach, following the little boy whom Manny had sent to find her.

Lars was still on the line when she climbed down the skimmer's top hatch. Manny was sitting in the pilot's seat; as she entered the cockpit, she observed that he'd patched himself directly into the com panel via a cable that he'd extended from his chest. "Here she is," Manny said, then he picked up the mike and extended it to her. "Lars. Says he's in trouble."

Marie hesitated, then took the mike from him. "Hello, Lars," she said, realizing even as she spoke how aloof she sounded. "How are you?"

"*Marie...oh, man, it's good to hear you.*" Although the satellite downlink should have been perfect, the signal was scratchy, fuzzed with static. "*I've got trouble. You gotta help me out.*"

Her lip curled. *What's the matter?* she was tempted to say. *Run out of bearshine and getting the shakes?* Yet when she glanced at Manny, he slowly nodded, confirming the gravity of the situation. "I'm listening...go on. Where are you?"

"*On the big river,*" he said, meaning the Great Equatorial River. "*About eighty miles southwest of you. An island a few miles west of the channel, just off the coast.*" His words came as a rush, and she was surprised to hear an undertone of panic in his voice. "*I'm not kidding. You gotta get down here...we need you, real bad.*"

"You've got a boat." Despite herself, she was still skeptical.

"*Sank. Shoals punched a hole in the hull while we were trying to make it to shore. We're lucky to get here before...*"

A sudden rush of sound, as something was moving past the satphone. In the background, a voice, unintelligible but nonetheless frightened. She caught only a few words— *"...back, get back, they might..."*—then Lars came back again.

"We've lost almost everyone." Now his voice was low, as if he was whispering into the satphone's mouthpiece. *"Just me, James, and Coop...and Coop's in bad shape. We've got only one gun, and that's not going to help much. Marie, swear to God, you gotta get us out of this."*

"Out of what?" Puzzled, she leaned closer to the com panel. "You're not making any sense. What's..."

Once again, in the background she hear a flurry of noise, as if the satphone was held in the hand of someone who was running. A couple swift, violent *pop-pop-pop* sounds that she immediately recognized as the semi-auto gunfire. Then Lars' voice returned *"Please, Marie...for the luvva God, come get us! I'm sorry about everything! Just come and..."*

A sudden snap, like a dry twig breaking. Then silence.

"I have a fix on the location." Manny disconnected the cable from the com panel and let it spool back into a panel within his chest. "Latitude three-point-one degrees north, twenty-three minutes, longitude seventy-seven-point-nine degrees west, nine minutes." He pointed to the comp screen above the yoke. "Here."

Marie peered at the screen. Displayed upon it was an orbital map of Coyote. As Manny indicated, the signal from Lars' satphone originated from the eastern tip of a large island off the southern coast of Great Dakota, just a few miles west of where the West Channel emptied into the Great Equatorial River.

She sighed. Less than a hundred miles away. Apparently Lars and his buddies hadn't wandered so far as she and the others thought they would. Maybe they thought they'd just go away for awhile, get in some drinking time and do a little fishing, then come home and sweet-talk their way back into good graces with everyone they'd left behind. She could almost imagine him now. *Oh, babe, I was just foolin' with you. You know how much I love you. C'mon, now, sweetie, just let me in...*

But that was in the past. She'd heard not only the gunshots, but also the terror in his voice. Somewhere just north of the equator, Lars had run into something that he couldn't handle. Marie tossed the mike on the dashboard, let out her breath.

"Better warm up the engines," she murmured. "I think we've going on a rescue mission."

They didn't go alone. When Marie went back into town to gather the things they'd need, she took a minute to find Chris and tell her what was going on. As it turned out, Missus Smith already knew something was up; the boy who'd fetched Marie had gone on to tell her as well, so when Marie located her in her cabin, she was putting her pack together.

"If there's trouble, you're going to need someone to ride shotgun." Chris didn't smile as she took down her rifle from the hooks above the door. Marie started to object, but she held up a hand. "James is a worthless drunk, and Cooper's a lowlife, but they're still my people. And you and Manny can't do this by yourselves."

Marie didn't argue. If the situation was as dire as Lars had led her believe, she knew they'd need all the help they could get. So the two of them grabbed a medkit and some food from the mess tent, then they hurried back to the beach. News traveled fast in Riverport; a small crowd had already gathered near the skimmer, wanting to know what was going on. Chris told them what little she and Marie knew, then gave the town's remaining satphone to another woman and told her to monitor the emergency frequency. If anything were to happen to them, Missus Smith said, she was to call to Liberty and request—no, demand—assistance from the Colonial Militia.

She and Marie climbed aboard the skimmer. Manny revved the engines, then put the fans in reverse and slowly backed out into the water. As the skimmer pulled away from shore, Missus Smith went below to join Manny in the cockpit; Marie lingered on the aft deck, though, and watched while Riverport receded from view. Once again, she was leaving home...and she found herself surprised to realize how much she'd come to regard this small, underpopulated settlement as home. Only last month, she'd thought it was a mistake to stop here. Now she was afraid she'd never see it again.

It took the rest of the day for them to travel down the coast. They'd left shortly before noon, and although the current was with them, the distance from Riverport to the delta where the West Channel emptied into the Great Equatorial River was considerable. Manny stayed close to shore as they cruised past the lowland marshes south of Riverport, vast tracts of sourgrass and spider bush, the southeast range of the Black Mountains rising beyond them. The humid air lay still, sullen in the warmth of the afternoon sun; skeeters purred around the aft deck, and from the shore they could hear the cries of nesting birds.

This was a part of the world none of them had ever seen before. It wasn't long, though, before the view became monotonous. Shortly after lunch, while Missus Smith took a siesta, Marie relieved Manny at the controls. Lars had been reluctant to let her drive the skimmer, so it was a pleasure to take the yoke, feel the smooth vibration of the fans beneath her hands. Despite the urgency of the mission, she throttled down a quarter-bar, just to savor the sensation of water passing swiftly beneath the bottom of the hull.

"Not in a rush, are you?" Manny said after a few minutes. "You can go faster, you know."

Marie glanced at him. "Just enjoying the ride, that's all."

"No apologies necessary." Manny turned his head to glance back at Missus Smith. She lay upon an unrolled sleeping bag in the aft compartment, eyes closed and hands folded together on her chest. "Day's getting short, and it looks rather tight for two people back there. Unless you want to sleep up top…"

Marie didn't reply, but instead throttled up the engines once more, returning the skimmer to cruise speed.

Through the canopy, she could make out a low ridge gradually falling toward the southeastern tip of Great Dakota. Just past that point lay the Great Equatorial River; somewhere beyond that, the island where Lars and his companions were shipwrecked.

"I don't get it," she murmured, keeping her voice low so Chris could sleep. "Lars has been gone...what, five, six weeks? And he gets stranded so close to us?" She shook her head. "What's he been doing all this time?"

"No idea." Manny hesitated. "What I'm more concerned about is what you're going to tell him when you see him again."

Marie didn't say anything. She hadn't given the subject much thought, believing that Lars was out of her life for good, or at least until after the baby was born. Indeed, no one in Riverport knew that she was pregnant, save for Manny. She hoped that, by the time her condition became obvious, the town would be self-sufficient enough that she could take maternity leave and return to Liberty long enough for Wendy to deliver the baby in the colonial hospital. Then she'd be able to go back to Great Dakota with her newborn child and a clear conscience that she'd done the right thing.

"As little as possible," she said after a moment. Then she gave him a sidelong frown. "And neither will you."

"My lips are sealed." A pause. "Literally."

Marie grinned at the self-effacing joke. "You'd make a great father, you know that?" A new thought occurred to her. "Think you'd like the job?"

Now it was Manny's turn to become silent. He didn't

respond for a minute or two; when Marie looked at him again, he was staring straight ahead, as if studying the channel. Once again, she found herself wishing that his face was capable of displaying emotion, so that she'd have an idea of what thoughts were passing through his mind.

"Stay close to shore," he said at last. "Get out into deep water, and you might have trouble with the current."

A couple of hours later, they left the West Channel and entered the Great Equatorial River.

It was almost twilight, the sun's reddish-orange light illuminating the enormous granite escarpment that marked the southeastern tip of Great Dakota. Like the prow of some mammoth, petrified vessel, the sharp-edged cliffs towered nearly three hundred feet above the jagged shoals below. Manny had taken the yoke back by then; carefully steering clear of the surf that crashed against the shoals, he slowed down so that they could take in the majesty of the giant rock. Missus Smith had awoken from her nap, and she and Marie stood on the aft deck, watching as the skimmer slowly cruised beneath its shadow.

Just past the delta was the Great Equatorial River, so broad that its far side lay beyond the horizon. To the east, on the opposite shore, they could make out the thin, dark line that marked the west coast of New Florida. It wasn't until Manny turned the skimmer to the west and they began traveling up the south coast of Great Dakota that they spotted the smoke. Back-lit by the setting sun, it curled upward as a slender tendril from a dark form that seemed to float upon the water.

The island...and someone there had lit a signal fire.

Wary of the fading light, Manny pushed the engines up to full throttle and switched on the spotlights. Salt spray drenched the aft deck, chasing the two women below; from the cockpit, they watched the island gradually grow larger. Now they could see that it was a narrow stretch of land, about five miles long but less than a mile across, and heavily forested. The smoke rose from the closer end of the island, yet they still couldn't see the fire. The island was a couple of miles away when the satphone crackled, and once again they heard Lars's voice.

"Hey, Marie! Is that you, babe?"

Marie picked up the handset. "Roger that. We see your smoke, and we're coming in."

Through the speaker, the ragged cheers of men shouting with relief. *"Oh, babe, I love you! Can't believe you got here so soon! Really made that sucker fly, didn'cha?"*

Marie glanced at Manny. "Don't let him know," he said quietly. "It'll just upset him."

Missus Smith snickered. Marie shook her head, then keyed the mike again. "Yeah, sure...look, the sun's going down, so you're going to have to help us find you. If you've got a light, turn it on and shine out toward the water so that we can see where you are."

A long pause, then Lars's voice returned, more calm this time. *"Can't do that. River horses might see it, follow it back to us. We're taking a chance as is, just keeping a fire going."*

"River horses?" Marie stared at the satphone in puzzlement. " What are you...?"

"Just take my word for it, okay? Kill your lights...we can see you now...and put someone on deck to look for the fire. That's where we are."

Marie shook her head, glanced at Manny. "What the hell is he...?"

"Never mind. I'll go." Rising from her seat, Chris picked up her carbine. "Just get us in close, and I'll yell as soon as I spot the beach."

"Chris, wait..."

"Don't worry about it. I got my best friend to protect me." Missus Smith patted the stock of her rifle, then ducked her head and left the cockpit.

Early evening had settled upon the river, with the first stars beginning to appear in the darkening sky, when they caught sight of a flickering glow upon the island's eastern tip, close to the waterline. Chris called down from the aft deck and Manny throttled back the engines, then swung around so that the skimmer approached the point from an oblique angle. Through the bubble, they could see the leading edge of Bear's rings appearing above the eastern horizon, casting a silver luminescence upon the black water.

A couple of sudden bumps against the bottom of the hull as the skimmer hit unseen driftwood. "Wish we could switch the spotlights," Marie murmured. "Can't see where we're going."

Manny turned off the interior lights. The cockpit was plunged into darkness save for the sallow glow of the instrument panel. "There," he said. "I can see now."

As if to demonstrate, he twisted the yoke hard to port. A moment later, there was gentle bump against the starboard pontoon as the skimmer grazed a floating log. Once again, Marie remembered that Manny possessed infrared vision; now that Bear was rising, he was able to use its light as human eyes could not. An uncomfortable reminder that Manny was a savant. His soul might be human, but his body was not.

"You're almost there!" Once more, Lars's voice crackled through the transceiver. *"C'mon in! We'll meet you at the water!"*

The fire was very close now, less than a few dozen yards away. Marie started to reach for the mike when Chris yelled down through the open top hatch. "There's something in the water! I saw it move!"

"Hold on!" Marie rose from her seat and started to head for the hatch. "I'm coming up!"

"Stay put." Manny remained calm. "We're almost there. Thirty feet more, and they'll be able to…"

A gunshot from the aft deck, followed by two more. Marie bolted from cockpit and scrambled up the ladder.

In the wan light cast from the open hatch, she saw Missus Smith standing at the starboard rail, rifle raised to her shoulder and pointed toward the water just beyond the skimmer. Left eye fixed upon the infrared sight, she tracked something Marie couldn't see, then cursed and raised the barrel.

"Dammit! It's gone under!" She glanced at Marie. "You see that?" Without waiting for an answer, she lunged for the far end of the deck, pointed the gun down over the side. "Whatever it is, it's goddamn big!"

"What did you see?" Marie peered into the darkness. With night closing in, there was little that her eyes could make out. "What did it look like?"

"I dunno." Missus Smith searched the water, her rifle's muzzle sweeping back and forth. "All I saw was this giant head. Sort of like a horse, but..."

"Hey! Over here!"

Lars's voice, from the port side. Looking around, Marie caught a brief glimpse of two figures caught in silhouette against the signal fire. Then they disappeared; a few seconds later, the sound of men splashing through shallow water, as if meaning to swim out toward the approaching skimmer.

"Stay back!" Marie rushed to the port rail as Manny coaxed the skimmer closer to shore. "There's something out...!"

Another gunshot from behind her, and Marie turned just in time to see a massive head rise above the starboard side.

Almost equine in shape, yet larger than horse's head she ever seen, it swayed back and forth upon a thick, amphibian neck. Narrow eyes deep within a bony skull reflected the dim glow of the fire light; she had an impression of jagged teeth inside a cavernous mouth, and shrank back in horror.

The river horse loomed above Missus Smith, and for a moment it seemed as if it was studying her. She squeezed off another shot, but her aim was wild. The creature recoiled, but only for an instant. Then its head pounced forward, and its jaws clamped down upon Chris's shoulder.

Crying out in agony, she dropped her weapon. The rifle clattered to deck, and Marie hurled herself toward it. Chris was battering her fists against the creature's skull as she snatched up the rifle.

"*Shoot it!*" Chris screamed. "*Shoot...!*"

Yet before Marie could get a clear shot, the creature yanked Chris from the deck. The toe of her left boot caught against the railing, and for a half-second Marie thought that might save her. Then the boot was ripped from her foot and her body was dragged overboard, down into the black water.

Marie ran to the railing, fired aimlessly into the water, but there was nothing to be done now; the river horse had disappeared, taking her friend with it.

She sagged against the railing, still staring at the place where Chris Smith had vanished. She was barely aware that Lars had scrambled up the ladder, with James just behind him, or that Manny had shoved the throttles all the way forward. The fans roared as the skimmer hurtled away from the island. Cold water, tasting of salt and death, cascaded upon her.

She stared back at the island that she'd barely visited, knowing even then that she'd never be the same again.

**From the diary of
Marie Montero:
Adnachiel 9, c.y. 06**

*We rescued Lars and James from Smith Island—that's
what Manny has decided to call it, in honor of Chris—but
they were the only two survivors. The other five men in
their group were killed by river horses: the first four in the
initial attack, with Cooper surviving long enough to reach
the island only to die before we could reach them. Considering everything that happened, they're lucky to be alive.*

*Lars wasn't pleased to see Manny again. Almost as
soon as he came aboard, in fact, he told Manny to hand
over the skimmer's controls. But Manny refused and I
backed him up, and after that Lars hunkered down in the
back with James. He didn't put up much of a fight, really.
He and James were cold, wet and hungry, and I think he
was more scared than he wanted to admit.*

*Took most of the night to get back home. Didn't
reach Riverport until a few hours before sunrise. Found
some food in the back (they'd lost everything when the
boat capsized...lucky that Lars had the satphone in his
pocket) and once they ate, Lars told us what happened.
Don't know how much is true and how much isn't, but
here goes:*

After they got thrown out, the seven of them sailed down a few miles downstream, then made camp in the swamps. At first they thought they'd just wait until "the heat blew over" (as Lars puts it), then come back and try to talk their way back into our good graces. After awhile, though, they decided that they were better off without us anyway—little did they know the feeling was mutual.

They knew they couldn't rough it on their own for very long, so they talked over what they should do next. Lars told them about his good friends in Bridgeton who he was sure would take him in—I remember when he tried to use that line on me—and he managed to persuade the others that everything would be wine and roses if they could only get there.

So they sailed down the West Channel to the Big River, then turned east and moved along the southern coast of New Florida, and finally turned north and went up the East Channel 'till they reached Bridgeton. Took them nearly three weeks to make the trip, so they must not have been in much of a hurry. James said something about "doing a lot of fishing." so I figure they were drinking all the way. Miracle they made it in the first place.

But they didn't stay long in Bridgeton before they had to move on again. Lars is a little vague about that part of the story. He says he found Tiny, Lester and Biggs, but none of them had room for the group in their houses and they couldn't find jobs anywhere, but I find that hard to believe. More likely that someone in town recognized Lars and knew that he'd been exiled from the colonies, and that taking him in would result in criminal prosecution. The way he carries on about how his pals "betrayed" him makes me wonder if his old buddies decided to play it safe and turn him in. Or maybe they just wore out their welcome, drinking and causing trouble, until everyone in town finally got fed up with them and the blueshirts showed them the way to the docks.

In any case, they left Bridgeton in a hurry. Now they had a choice—either keep going north and try for New Boston (fat chance! they would've gotten the same reception there, more than likely!) or go back the way they'd come and try to beg forgiveness from Missus Smith.

That's when Lars turned on his charm. For the next few minutes, I got an earful about how much he loved me, how he couldn't live without me, etc. while James is sitting beside him with this shit-eating grin on his face, staring down the front of my shirt. I heard him out, then told him to go on with the story.

So, anyway, they sailed back down the East Channel until they reached the big river, then turned west and started toward Great Dakota. But they'd just reached the delta and were about to turn north up the West Channel when they changed their minds and instead decided to go downriver a little further.

Again, I'm not sure what to believe. Lars says that some of the others wanted to get in a little more fishing, while James says they wanted to give us a little more time to think about how much they missed us. I think the truth is somewhere in-between—i.e. they got cold feet about having to beg their way back into camp. Besides, the weather was still warm and they still had plenty of booze (no doubt they picked up more bearshine in Bridgeton). In any case, they opted to sail downriver a little ways—to have one more party before they came home to face the music, I think—to an island they'd spotted before.

That's when the river horses found them.

There's a lot about Coyote we still don't know, even after being here nearly nineteen Earth-years. Not all of it is the same; we're still finding new animals, plants, etc. And considering how long the Great Equatorial River is, we've barely explored 1/10th of it. So maybe we shouldn't be surprised that there's more to it than catwhales, weirdlings and redfish...creatures that have never met humans before, and don't care if we've got boats and guns.

In any case, the boat was coming close to the island when they attacked. Lars says that Cooper gave them the name "river horses" because they look like sea horses back on Earth, only bigger (yeah—a lot bigger). Manny believes the similarity may only come from what they saw above water; he thinks they may be something like crocodiles back on Earth, only warm-blooded and much larger. That's something I don't know, though, so I have to take his word for it.

In any case, a pack of them attacked the boat just as the men approached the island. Two or maybe three of them came in all at once, from both sides, just after one of the guys jumped overboard to swim ashore with a rope to tie off. He died first, before the rest of the group knew what hit him, and while the others were still running back and forth on deck, the other two went for the boat.

It's hard to tell to what happened after that, except that everyone panicked. The flechette guns they had were useless, in any case. Three more men were killed and the boat capsized before Lars, James and Cooper managed to swim ashore. And even then Coop barely got away—a river horse caught him in its mouth, but he kicked it in some way that made it let him go (I wish Chris had learned that trick) then Lars grabbed him and hauled him ashore. By then their friends were gone and their boat was sunk.

Like I said, they were lucky on two scores: Lars was carrying the satphone in his shirt pocket and James had a waterproof lighter in his pants. So after they carried Cooper the rest of the way onto dry land, they started a fire on the beach. But that seemed to attract the river horses, so they doused it, and didn't start another one until after Lars used the satphone to call for help and they were sure we were on the way. They tried to keep Coop alive, but they didn't have a med kit and he'd lost too much blood. By the time we got to them, he'd been dead three hours.

Don't know what to make of all this. Lars is back. He's asleep in my bed in the cabin I built without his help. When he gets up, maybe I'll talk to him. Or maybe I won't. But he's not welcome, that's for damn sure.

River horses. What a name. Kind of think it describes me. Something that just keeps pulling and pulling, with no end in sight.

Marie kept her distance from Lars. As soon as she could, she evicted him from her cabin, telling him that, despite what happened on Smith Island, she wasn't taking him back. No one else in town wanted him either, so he and James moved into a tool shed, the only shelter available to them in Riverport.

The two men found jobs with the timber crew, and for a little while it seemed as if Marie would be able to keep Lars out of her life. They saw each other infrequently, usually at dinner time when they stood in the chow line together, and her friends made sure that she never had to sit next to him. It hardly mattered, though, because Lars seldom spoke to her; indeed, his only companion was James, and together they occupied the lowest rung of the social ladder. Although they'd returned to the settlement, they were far from being accepted back into the community. Everyone knew what had occurred on Smith Island, and they held Lars and James responsible for Missus Smith's death.

Yet it wasn't long before the situation changed.

With Chris gone, there was a vacuum that had to be filled. Although Marie didn't want the job, she soon found the others turning to her for leadership. She and Missus Smith had been close, and people were looking for someone who could fill her role. So it came to pass that, when the next town meeting rolled around and a special election was held, Marie discovered she was the sole nominee for mayor. Although she accepted the job with reluctance, she promised to continue the work her predecessor had begun, the transformation of Riverport into a self-sufficient community.

By then, that which only Manny had known had become obvious: she was pregnant, with her child due by the end of the year. Now that she was mayor, Marie knew leaving Riverport even for a short while was out of the question. Yet she also realized that her condition gave the settlement a bargaining chip it hadn't possessed before. So one evening, with Manny's assistance, she composed a formal letter to the Colonial Council, which was transmitted via satphone to Liberty the following morning.

The response came quickly, and not the way she'd expected. Marie was working on the farm when she heard a familiar sound. Turning to raise a hand against the afternoon sun, she watched as a gyro soared across the West Channel, making a lazy arch above the settlement as the pilot searched for a place to land. Marie put down her rake, picked up her straw hat from where she'd placed it on a tree stump, and walked back into town to greet the visitors.

She wasn't surprised to find that the delegation from Liberty included Carlos. For a few seconds after he climbed out of the gyro, brother and sister regarded one another with mutual discomfort, neither of them quite knowing what to say or do. Then Carlos grinned and stretched out his hands, and Marie walked over to give him a hug, to the warm applause of the settlers who'd come out to the beach.

This wasn't the only reunion. Also aboard the gyro was Clark Thompson. He waited patiently beside the aircraft until his nephew shuffled forward from the back of the crowd. Lars was a broken man; thin and hollow-eyed, his shoulders slumped, he'd lost the arrogance that he had carried when he'd left New Florida. The two men regarded each other for a moment, then Clark solemnly extended his hand, and Lars took it with shame-faced reticence.

The townspeople quit work early that afternoon, and a special dinner was prepared for their honored guests. While the cooks labored in the mess tent, Marie escorted Carlos and Clark, along with the two other members of the Council, on a quick tour of Riverport. Although she was embarrassed by what little she had to show them—a half-dozen log cabins, along with a couple of sheds and a half-build greenhouse—the council representatives were impressed by the progress made in only a month by less than thirty people. It was clear, though, that the settlement would need assistance if it was going to survive the long winter ahead, and Marie knew without asking that this support would not come without a price.

Her suspicions were confirmed shortly after dinner, when Carlos came over to her. "Let's take a walk, shall we?" he said quietly. "There's some things we need to discuss, just the two of us."

The crimson rays of the setting sun peered from behind purple clouds as they strolled together along the beach, Marie's hand clasped within the crook of Carlos's arm. "You've done well," he said as they walked along the water's edge, watching the tide lap at the mottled sands. "Better than I thought...than we thought...you would."

"Thank you." To the east. Bear's ring-plane was beginning to glide into view above the horizon. "I can't take credit for this, though. These people have worked awful hard to..."

"I don't mean the colony. I mean you." He pulled her a little closer. "Hard to believe you're the same girl...the same woman, I mean...who was getting in bar fights just a month ago. You've changed a lot since then. I'm proud of you."

"Well..."

"Hear me out, please. This is important." He paused, as if to choose his words. "I've spoken with the magistrates. They're willing to let you return...on probation, at least, so long as you behave yourself...but my guess is that you won't come back."

"Nope." Marie grinned and shook her head. "Wouldn't look good for a mayor to skip town just because she's pregnant. " Her smile faded. "Besides, people might think I'm nothing but trouble. Can't have that, can we?" Embarrassed, Carlos looked away. He started to release her arm, but she pulled him close again. "Forget it. You did what you had to do. If you didn't, I'd be digging ditches now."

"Yeah, well...like I said, you did better than most people expected." He glanced back at the settlement. "As for Lars...that's a whole 'nother issue."

"Not an issue at all." Marie gazed out at the channel. "He's got his life now, and I've got mine. So far as I'm concerned, he can go back any time he wants. We'll get along just fine without him."

"Well...no." Carlos shook his head. "The amnesty the maggies have offered you doesn't extend to him. They know everything he did...or at least what you've told us, along with how he tried to hide out in Bridgeton...and they don't consider him to be—" he searched for the correct phrase "—'sufficiently rehabilitated,' if I remember it correctly. So he's stuck here, whether he likes it or not."

"All right." Marie gave an offhand shrug. "Fine. Whatever makes them happy, I can live with it."

"It's a little more complicated than that." Carlos let go of her arm, tucked his hands in his pockets. "Problem is, you're carrying his child. And Uncle Clark is an old-fashioned sort of guy who seems to think that, no matter what else, his nephew has a right to be a father."

"Like hell, he does." Feeling a surge of anger, Marie stopped and turned toward him. "Lars knocked me up one night when I was too tired to resist. He..."

"Did he rape you?" Carlos looked her straight in the eye. "Tell the truth."

She hesitated. "Well, no, but..."

"Then there's nothing I can do...and please, don't ask me to lie on your behalf." He held up a hand before she could object. "Clark Thompson hasn't given up on his boy, any more than I gave up on you. He wants the best for him, and that includes the prospect of him settling down and raising a family."

"Oh, for the love of..."

"Just listen, please." Carlos let out his breath. "There's more to this than just you two. Clark has a strong voice on the Council, and it's become even stronger since word came that you and Lars discovered a new source of timber..."

"It wasn't him and me, dammit." She felt her face becoming warm. "It was Chris Smith's idea. She..."

"Maybe, but she's not around anymore, is she? And the way Clark has put this to the council, this is your settlement. Yours and Lars's." Again, he raised a hand before she could protest. "He's willing to allocate everything you need...tools, generators, boats, whatever...to turn this place into a viable colony as soon as possible. A blank check..."

"But his signature has to be on it." Marie stared at him. "Right?"

"Right." Carlos bent down to pick up a piece of driftwood. "But that's just council business. I've also learned that he's already taken steps toward setting up a private company to corner the market on the Great Dakota timber industry. The Thompson Wood Company, with him and Molly in control..."

"Oh, great. That's excellent." Marie shook her head in disgust. "Coyote's first major corporation. What's next, a stockholder meeting?"

"Probably." Carlos hurled the stick out into the water. "What do you want? Social collectivism all over again? Maybe Manny Castro would like that, but..."

"Leave Manny out of this." She absently ran her fingers through her hair. "Look, let me get this straight. Clark is willing to provide support for Riverport..."

"Which is what you want."

"...but he's not going to persuade the Council to give us the stuff we need to do that unless his family has a lock on the timber industry."

"That's correct, yes."

"And for him to do that, he wants..." Marie's voice trailed off as she put everything together. "Oh, god... Carlos, you can't be saying..."

"You know what I'm saying." Carlos looked down at the ground, suddenly reluctant to meet her eyes. "Uncle Clark wants what's best for his favorite nephew. A wife, a child, a job..."

"I don't love him!" In frustration, she turned away from him. "He's not the one I want! I...!"

She stopped before she said something she knew she'd regret. Her legs buckled beneath her, and she fell on bended knees to the beach. "Is there someone else?" Carlos asked, kneeling down beside her. "Who is it? Tell me, please...."

Marie raised her head, looked away. For just a moment, beyond the nearest dune, she caught a glimpse of a figure in cloaked in shadows, a single red eye reflecting the light of the setting sun. Then the figure disappeared, a twilight ghost swallowed by the coming night.

"No," she whispered. "There's no one else."

From the diary of
Marie Montero:
Barbiel 15, c.y. 06

The first keelboat from Liberty arrived today: fifteen people in all, including Clark and Molly Thompson and Lars' brother Garth. And that's just one boat: two more are on the way, sailing out from Bridgeton and making their way around New Florida until they reach Great Dakota. We've made sure that they know to avoid Smith Island. That place belongs to the river horses, and we stay away from there.

By the time everyone gets here, Riverport's population will have doubled—no, tripled—in size. Only a couple of months ago, this would've been unimaginable. Maybe even impossible: there was no way we could have supported seventy-two people. But apparently there's quite a few folks in New Florida and Midland who want to take a shot at starting a new colony, especially if there's an excellent chance they'll make a good living working for the Thompson Wood Company.

Now that the Council has formally recognized us, we're getting everything we need: food, livestock, clothing, hardware, building materials, comps, even a couple of electrical generators. I was told that several panes of uncut plate glass are also being shipped out to us, which means we'll be able to finish work on the greenhouse. Such a small thing, really, and yet so necessary. Once the greenhouse is up, we'll be able to feed ourselves through winter.

Lars is happier now that he has his family with him. Our relationship has been pretty much touch and go since he moved in with me. Even though I've told him that he's going back to the tool shed if he starts drinking again, there's been a couple of nights when he's come home with ale on his breath. Decided to look past that as much as I can. He's been nicer to me lately. And he seems to be honestly looking forward to raising a child. We've already decided on names: Hawk if it's a boy, Rain if it's a girl.

Clark insists that we get married, and I think that's pretty much inevitable. I'm still not sure whether I can love Lars, but the baby is coming soon, and he or she is going to need a daddy. Besides, the Thompson Wood Company is going to be a family-owned business. If I want an interest in it, getting hitched to Lars is part of the deal. Carlos and Wendy still don't trust him very much, but they're willing to go along with the plan. It may not be the happiest of marriages, but...well, we'll see.

Clark and I have talked things over lately, and we've agreed that he's probably better cut out to be mayor than I am. After all, he's had experience with this sort of thing before, and with a baby on the way, the last thing I need to worry about is running a town. We haven't gone public *with this yet, but once all the newcomers arrive and get settled in, I'm going to resign and put my support behind him in the special election. Maybe not the most democratic way of doing things, but at least it'll help make sure that Riverport has a strong leader during its first year.*

So all is well, or at least as well as it can be. Except for one thing...

anuel Castro had his own cabin, a one-room shack on the far side of town. A handful of New Boston settlers helped him build it, but since then he'd lived alone, becoming increasingly reclusive as new people began to arrive in Riverport. The cabin had no windows, and no any furniture save a table, a chair, and a cabinet for his few belongings. The only room was lit by a fish-oil lamp suspended from its rafters, and it wasn't until that someone noticed that they didn't see its glow seeping beneath the doorframe one evening that anyone realized the savant had disappeared.

Learning this news the following morning, Marie hurried to his cabin, only to discover it had been stripped bare. Manny hadn't left a note, yet when she questioned several townspeople, she discovered that he'd recently bartered his meager possessions—his chair here, his desk there—in exchange for hand tools and a backpack. The sort of things one might need in order to homestead in the wilderness. That was when she knew where he'd gone.

She didn't tell Lars or anyone else where she was going when she left town by herself. By then it was late autumn; the wind had long since ripped the leaves from the trees, and the first hard freeze had solidified the ground. She bundled herself warmly in the oversized wool serape a couple of friends had woven for her, and filled a water-skin from the town well. Along the way, she found a broken tree limb to use as a staff to help support her weight. In her second trimester, it felt as if she were carrying a heavy sack in her midriff; she made sure that she rested frequently, and drank water whenever she was thirsty.

The path leading into the foothills was just as she'd remembered it, when she and Manny had hiked up Thunder Ridge in the first days of autumn. The season had become colder since then, the sky the color of iron, yet by midday she'd reached the bluff where she and Manny had rested on an afternoon more warm and fair than this, and it was here that she found him.

It was almost as if he'd never left this place at all. He sat on a boulder, pad propped upon his knee, using a claw-like finger to etch a picture on its screen. His cowl was pulled up around his face, though, so his blind eye didn't see her coming until her staff made a scraping noise on bare rock. Then he looked up, and he stared at her for a long time.

"Marie," he said at last. "You shouldn't have come."

"You shouldn't have left." She clung to the branch with both hands, trying to catch her breath. "Damn it, Manny. Why did you...?"

"Hush." Putting down his pad, he rose to his feet and walked over to her. "You're pregnant, remember? This can't be good for..."

"I'm fine. Exercise is good for the baby." Yet she let him take her by the shoulders, ease her to a seat on the ground. "Where do you think you're going? Why didn't you...?"

"So many questions." The soft rasp from his chest that signified a chuckle. "You know, you've changed quite a bit since we first met. Back then..."

"Shut up and talk to me."

"Which do you want first? Shut up, or...?"

"Never mind." She glared at him. "Why...?"

"Because I don't belong down there." His single eye peered at her. "I went with you and Lars because I didn't want to be the resident freak in Liberty. Now Lars is back, and I don't want to be the resident freak in Riverport either."

"Lars is..."

"I know what Lars is, just as I know that I can't compete with him." He shook his head. "I need to find my own place in the world, even if it means living alone. So I left. Simple solution to a simple problem," All this came in the same monotone he'd assumed when he'd first met her. "Any more questions? Catch your breath, and..."

"One more, then I'll go home." She stared at him. "Do you love me?"

"Of course, I love you." His reply was immediate, without reservation. "You should know that by now, just as you know it'll never work out..."

"Dammit, Manny...!"

"Please...just listen." Standing up, he pointed toward the nearby hills. "I'm building a cabin up there. Just for myself, with no one else around. But if you ever need me, that's where I'll be."

She tried hard not to cry, but the tears came anyway. Manny didn't say anything for a moment, then he reached down and, taking her by the shoulders, gently raised her to her feet. "You'll do fine. You've got a family again, and you're no longer an outcast. Everything you've ever wanted is yours for the taking. All you need to do is be strong...and you've shown that you have more courage than you thought you had."

She started to reply, but found that she could think of nothing to say, so instead she put her arms around Manny and lay her head against his chest. She heard no heartbeat within his metallic body, yet when he wrapped his arms around her shoulders, the embrace was tender and undeniably human.

They stood that way for a long time until he finally pushed her away. Looking up at him, she was surprised to see a few white flakes upon his cowl; unnoticed by either of them, snow had begun to fall.

"Storm's coming in," she murmured. "I better get back."

"Yes, you should." Manny reached down, picked up her walking stick. "Go quickly, before it gets too rough."

Marie nodded as she took the stick from him. There was nothing more to be said, so she turned and started toward the downhill trail. At the edge of the tree line, though, she paused to look back. The snow was falling more swiftly now, making a soft hiss as the wind carried it through the trees.

For a moment, she caught a last glimpse of a black-robed figure walking across the bluff, heading for the dense woodlands. And then he was gone, leaving her to follow a path that was hers and hers alone.